I0656063

DiaryUnlimited.com

www.DiaryUnlimited.com

Design and Layout by Tom Norwood

DEDICATION

TO WHOM IT MAY CONCERN

The Y2K File

featuring:
The Y2K Diary

by

Old Nick and Tom Norwood

CONTENTS

The Diary of the year 2000.

Contents

Nothing is what it seems

ACKNOWLEDGMENTS

Nothing is what it seems…

1 THE YEAR 2000

The following pamphlet is a series of entries into a web diary which started on the first of January 2000 and became an important think tank with its 120 000 registered users. We, you, he, she, they became I with an urge to communicate the underlying causes and torments of a parallel universe. I live in the positive dimension and within it there is this negative universe. It is like an unprocessed or negative image in analogue photography. No time zones, no geographical borders and no restrictions. Everyone is everyone and refers to as I; I communicate; therefore, I live.

I created a search engine in order to retrieve the previous entries and eventually the future and present entries thus erasing the distance between the concept of time and its user. As the user started to get hooked and sucked into the system it became the punishment. As more entries unravelled the truth, the user entered into a cycle of incessant torture.

I'm past the present tense. I'm living in the present Tense; I've passed the present tense in the Past of the Present Tense. Not all the present was composed. Just past the present tense. Things did happen, no one will deny or disagree with this and any events are fully traceable, searchable.

On the first of January, I thought we simply ought to commemorate the millennium, even if the precise date was only true for a tiny minority on this earth. I created the "Y2K Diary". I started a diary. What is really astounding is the sheer scale at which I've managed to put together this entity: the "Y2K Diary.com" where murders are resolved and where swindlers get stoned. I was- I'm- this "Unbearable Lightness of Being" chasing this "Great Swindle of Being".

I never pretended to make any sense. Just to portray an exit to oblivion. To mystify what is deemed not suitable for the marketers of common literature.

One million hits for an anti-virus device: easier to get users in this way under a false pretence but harder to retain them. Incidentally I was an anti-virus of some sort. Some 200 000 stayed, a year on 100 000 deserted me. I win some and I lose some. Three years on, about 130 000 tuned in every month.

After the first year, the profile of my users was divided as follows: 468 076 users. After the third month of activity I started to engage the users into revealing their most private details. I can never tell the reliability of the response, but my 6th sense tells me that the majority were quite willing to tell the truth. My media profile ranged from their age group, occupation, habits, and hobbies to sexual practices. I received many queries, many desperate quests for solutions. I became the ultimate problem solver. The Diary confirmed what I knew all along that I'm living a constant civil war with life and with very unscrupulous devils.

I began to realise how lawless my society really is and when there is little hope around, this becomes the 'Great Swindle of Being'. I became a watchdog and a think tank. I confronted the devils of this world and most of them were quite willing to provide an answer. Most completely ignored me and instead sent me some gift vouchers. I became a billionaire in gift vouchers. Still their answers are incredibly valuable.

There are so many people telling me what to do and not to do all the time. All the bloody fuckers for whom life is poisoned to the core makes us wonder if it is worth living at all.

If everything I buy is doubtful, what is left for me to consume? I need some options and I want some real choices. I want the right to rid the world of these people telling me who I am supposed to be.

The author who wrote the novel Crime and Punishment deserves a paean of eulogies for contributing to the most self-inflicting punishment of all: torture or mental masturbation. Seeing, witnessing and depicting the horrors and misfortunes of life with any sense of irony is a crime in itself. It is not about being indifferent in the face of someone else's agony and desperation, but merely realistic in the face of adversity. Sadomasochism is the most popular indulgence of the late 20th century and beginning of the next. Come to think of it, since the advent of mankind on the planet. To corroborate my point, I created this Internet portal. The idea behind was to engage the rest of the world into a game of reality news. Launched on the day the earth was supposed to stand still, the Y2K. Every day I interacted and compiled the news as it came along. It wasn't necessarily a reaction to a real event, but a question. I was asked questions and I was supposed to answer. I was the one knowing all the answers. I didn't know all the answers so I instead triggered more questions and the questions in turn became more questions which then in turn became even more questions and so on and so forth. History was being recreated. With hindsight, I realise that the questions from the questions of the questions from the previous questions became the answers. The story is a long crime novel; the plot is being resolved but without the means or the will to eradicate any of the crimes committed.

Anyone who thought I was running out of time had been wrong. Time is just an optical illusion.

Time
1. Time. Lost in the dust of time.
2. Time. What time is it?
3. Time. Time to take a cigarette...
4. Time. And the passing time...
5. Time. It's time to go.
6. Time. I haven't got the time.

7. http://www.swatch.com/internettime has been adopted already by most US-based web sites from Apple to CNN. Swatch divides the day into 1000 beats. One beat equals one minute, 26.4 seconds. Noon = 500 beats. Internet Time represents a completely new global concept of time. Swatch beat; the revolutionary new unit of time means the following: No Time Zones No Geographical Borders.

How long is a Swatch beat? In short it has been divided up the virtual and real day into 1000 "beats". One Swatch beat is the equivalent of 1 minute 26.4 seconds. That means that 12 noon in the old-time system is the equivalent of @500 Swatch beats.

8. http://newearthtime.net/hippy time, where the day is divided into 360 degrees. 360 Earth beats every day, 1 earth beats every day, 15 earth beats in an hour and one earth beats

every four minutes.

9. a) Time to the meridian of Paris (1891). b) Time to the Greenwich meridian (1911) -Greenwich Mean Time-. GMT time delays the previous one from 9 min 21 s and has been designated to be the Universal Time. c) Time from Central Europe (in WW2) forward one hour from GMT.

10. I'm hardly a good timekeeper. I don't wear a watch, never have been and never will. I just can't. Anyway, I have a psychological notion of time. I can't measure up to the minute; the second but I round it up every two hours. I measure the tempo of my music when I practise an instrument. That's about the only time I dare to interfere. No one invades my time without my approval. (Theoretically) Time can be easily challenged and regained. It's only a matter of knowing when to stop and break with the treadmill of life.

And again: No Time Zones. No Geographical Borders. Back and again: No Time Zones. No Geographical Borders.

Back and forth, let us search…

January

entry date: 01.01.00

1. "The Diary is Open"

Welcome to the Y2K years.

We've made it! We're in 00.

We can start again. Everything has been forgiven.

Some are still celebrating on their own in an empty Dome, a symbol of fiascos and money wastage, an insult to all the worthy causes they could have generated instead.

Now that the bug didn't strike after all, we just have to wait for Y2K1 to see the outcome.

Bookmark the Y2K Showcase and Diary now.

One entry a day.

Feel free to submit an entry or reply to an entry.

Happy 00 Bug!

entry date: 02.01.00

2. "A Diary"

Another page in my diary.

A journal.

An almanack.

A piece of life.

You're reading one.

entry date: 03.01.00

3. "Online Music"

NME >>>> Mp3, Mp4, Mp5, Mp6 etc.

Yahoo Online >>>> It means…

Download Music >>>> …That…

MP3 music to download   >>>> …whoever…

Music, chat, links >>>> …controls…

More MP3 >>>> …the website…

Launch >>>> …will control…

MTV >>>> …the sale and…

VH1 >>>> …the ratings!

entry date: 04.01.00

4. "Mnemonics"

When we hear the first noun, we mentally picture the thing it represents and relate this, by interactive imagery, to the first landmark.

We are free to devise whatever interactive imagery best suits us, but the more animated and distinctive, the better. Having thus associated the first noun and (locus), we dismiss the scene from mind, and deal likewise with the second noun and the second locus, and so on.

related links:

Follow the end of the path:

mnemonic techniques

mnemonics.com

mnemonics.org

entry date: 05.01.00

5. "Direction"

The compass.

entry date: 06.01.00

6. "Direction (Part 2)"

The labyrinth.

entry date: 07.01.00

7. "The World of Mushrooms"

related links:

Wild mushrooms - The Good, the Bad and the Ugly.

Fungal Jungal - Testing your knowledge of mushrooms.

A Message board and links.

A criminal case involving magic mushrooms.

Magic mushrooms - Enter at your own risk!

entry date: 08.01.00

8. "POP Culture"

Defines popular art accessible for the masses, but only understood by those who conceived it.

entry date: 09.01.00

9. "ART 2000"

ART. I hate that word because it is pretentious.

It doesn't do much for painting, sculpture, design or any kind of self-expression. We should remove this word from our vocabulary.

ART is no means of describing beauty but an artefact and a metaphor of a hidden identity.

So there!

ART 2000 is the national fair for visual arts coming to London at the Business Design Center in Islington.

Two weeks of display with amazing painting, sculpture and

electronic art. One can contemplate and even buy. Prices range from £100 to £20,000.

related links:

For more information:

 visit the Business Design Center online.

entry date: 10.01.00

10. "New York, New York"

I'm from New York and I think it is time to (re-)discover the parks.

Everyone should expect my list to get bigger and bigger. I'm also working on one for London.

related links:

This is my park.

entry date: 11.01.00

11. "The Morse Alphabet

Binary language. Day one.

entry date: 12.01.00

12. "Space"

related links:

NASA - Windows to the Universe.

Cape Canaveral, all you need to know about our Universe.

NASA Resource Centre. Space Calendar, Space FAQ.

An online version of the film Map of the Universe.

entry date: 13.01.00

13. "The Stock Market"

E-World.com

E-Commerce.com

E-War.com

entry date: 14.01.00

14. "Numbers (part 1)"

Our numbers emulate the Arabic alphabet.

In the digital age, 10 is the norm and 13 is either bad luck or a good luck number.

We live in numbers and for numbers.

We would not have survived without them.

They compute our very own existence.

entry date: 15.01.00

15. "Numbers"

related links:

Maths

Programming numbers

Number translator

Decimal to Hexadecimal Conversion Table

entry date: 16.01.00

16. "Symbols"

related links:

Religious symbols.

The film, Map of the Universe, uses symbols –heavily-.

Symbolic meaning of the Six-Pointed Star in various

traditions.

Perfection of the art of symbolism in Hinduism.

They will sell you a book about it.

Symbols in Christian Arts and Architecture.

Graphical Symbols Compliant to IEC 417 Ed.1

entry date: 17.01.00

17. "I'm Getting Married"

Ding Dong! I'm getting married today!

This sacrosanct family value has apparently caught up with me.

Maybe I'm getting old.

My man to be is eight years younger than myself and happens to be my work mate Tom Norwood. We're already working on the children to be.

Our witnesses will be Nick and Janet, they are both working with me. We're planning a lavish ceremony today at 2PM GMT in Hoxton Square, London N1.

related links:

Ugly Wedding cards at Yahoo, don't send me any from that lot!

I'm not trying to plug in Yahoo or anything, but there are some hilarious straight and gay wedding experiences there.

A wedding page with a funeral theme tune? Go for it!

Pranks can be seen in 5 languages and are a bit cheesy.

Everything you need to know for a proper and clean marriage. JD

entry date: 18.01.00

18. "I'm Getting Divorced"

False alarm! It was all a bad, bad dream. I'm still single.

It was a nightmare generated as a result of an overindulgence of Stella-Artois and Smirnoff. My heartiest apologies for all those who turned up on Hoxton square on Saturday afternoon, overfilling the square to capacity.

It would have been a memorable wedding, though when I think of it: if I would have been married by mistake, what could I have done next?

related links:

Don't get married.

What happens when a child wants a divorce?

Questioning the failed marriages of generation X.

entry date: 19.01.00

19. "Water"

related links:

Image taken from the film: Map of the Universe.

Don't flush it! Campaign for saving rivers.

entry date: 20.01.00

20. "Communication"

related links:

An intercultural search engine, messages, forum, and courses from around the world.

entry date: 21.01.00

21. "Silence"

Breaking the silence.com.

A website absents for many years.

Under construction.

related links:

The war against silence.

Where has all the silence gone?

Devoted to poems inspired by the Holocaust.

The Day of Silence project; education against homophobia.

Deaf World Point, resources and links.

A zone for deaf people and the hard of hearing.

E-deaf people in the UK.

entry date: 22.01.00

22. "Y2K Elements"

Images taken from the film Map of the Universe.

entry date: 23.01.00

23. "Science"

Mary and John, age 5 and 8. They both live in London.

- What's your science?   [Mary]

- What's yours?   [John]

- I've asked the question.   [Mary]

- Science yourself!   [John]

- I've got no science.   [Mary]

- You do it, don't you?   [John]

- Yeah?   [Mary]

- There you go!   [John]

Eating is a science.

entry date: 24.01.00

24. "Past Tense"

entry date: 25.01.00

25. "Present Tense"

= + .

entry date: 26.01.00

26. "Future Tense"

entry date: 27.01.00

27. "If, But and Maybe"

"If and ififififif, no but but but but, maybe, if only. "

As seen almost everywhere in recent weeks in newspapers, magazine, on the radio and on TV.

Why do we do it? Why are we rambling on?

'IF' signals a profound sense of desperation, alienation.

"If only the world was a better place!"

Of course, it would be better would it not?

It isn't. No buts. No maybe, no artificial tea-room small-talk. One makes one's bed. Everyone must generate enough will power to retract to one's sentiment of regrets. Regrets are synonymous with negativity. Negativity doesn't make the world go around, does it? **So there!**

entry date: 28.01.00

28. "Red"

entry date: 29.01.00

29. "Orange"

An orange can be viewed, eaten, bought, sold and anyone can communicate with it.

The orange colour was not long ago only used in advertising as an unresolved time-delayed compromise.

Sainsbury's supermarket from the late sixties and early seventies when orange was a must in colouring.

Now it seems to have gathered momentum since the late nineties.

Orange mobile communications, EasyJet and the list seems to be endless.

An almost unseen and unpronounced word in the eighties, too reminiscent of an era that the then fashion hoped to forget.

Now, it is a revival in one form or another.

It is suddenly no longer dated and very populist indeed.

Fa-fa-fa-fa-fa-fashion!

entry date: 30.01.00

30. "Books and Grimoires (ancient books)"

It is said that books will never disappear and the same could be said for all the *grimoires* (French: ancient books) lost in the dust of time.

A book is an artefact. A commodity. A pleasure.

Some say knowledge.

A *grimoire* was the original hand-written book used by magicians. One can buy books online. We use Amazon.com and when I can't find the one I really want I go for AltaVista and if by a stroke of bad luck, I can't find it there, I then hurtle along to my favourite bookshop.

I need books. I read them, swallow them and digest them. I often repeat that exercise many times over. I use the web a lot. It's similar, but different.

A book can be interactive too, depending on which angle you're looking at. It's peaceful. It's a sanctuary. It's losing one's mind (has to be a good book.) I've read a few that made me sweat for all the poor trees that have been chopped down in the process. It's rare, though.

entry date: 31.01.00

31. "Elements of the Universe"

Images taken from the film Map of the Universe.

February

entry date: 01.02.00

32. "What Do They Do?"

In time we do get to meet and work with a lot of people from mixed backgrounds. Some have achieved so much and I can't even begin to reach their level. My bookmark list is getting bigger and better.

I will start from the beginning:

Eye4U,

Absurd,

Map of the Universe,

Cyril,

Believe,

Zoonzone,

Miles,

Wrong Bodies.

To be continued...

entry date: 02.02.00

33. "What Really Bugs Me"

What really bugs me is when a newspaper, TV or advert mentions either:

a) a wrong URL,

b) an obsolete URL,

c) a wrong email,

d) an obsolete email,

e) keeps on advertising it for weeks-on-end, without a care in the world.

It happens!

It was at epidemic levels in January and it was truly ugly and irritating.

entry date: 03.02.00

34. "Ordering Roses Online"

related links:

Ordering online

entry date: 04.02.00

35. "Moaning"

Garlic is good for the heart and blood pressure.

Chamomile tea is vital for a perfect blood circulation, whilst onions restore a perfect digestion system and clean the whole body.

"Moaning is good for the depraved and the uneducated," preaches my colleague Tom.

I like moaning, not in excess though.

I do state when things are wrong and must be changed.

I put my moaning to positive uses. I do not moan for the sake of moaning. My name is not Julie Burchill. If the latter makes a living out of it, I'm still doing it to change the world.

A good moan is healthy.

entry date: 05.02.00

36. "Organic"

From an organic shampoo which only shares the name but is

completely devoid of any intrinsic values. Organic mushrooms from the supermarket Tesco tasting like wet sponge and apples from Sainsbury's screaming about how tasteless they are.

All having the stamp of approval from the

Organic Association.

So what does it mean? Very little in fact!

As it implies that no chemicals have been pumped into it.
Besides, due to the growing demand, they all become mass
produced and therefore, not really organic.

I was fortunate enough to grow up near a garden and we
always had tons of organic vegetables to eat. I can taste the
difference. I can also taste it in the price, though if most of the
range is still far cheaper than the troubled supermarket Marks
and Spencer, still charging over the odds for fresh but non-
organic foods, over-wrapped to capacity with plastic and
paper to demonstrate fresher freshness.

Fresh doesn't work anymore. A once upon a time stepping
stone in advertising mottos, now it wouldn't mean "diddly
squat."

It seems that organic is now wearing the brunt of the same
controversy.

entry date: 06.02.00

37. "The Moon. A Tourist Guide of the Satellite"

The moon, a satellite, not a planet is responsible for all the
traumas we endure. By circling around our planet Earth, the

moon is affecting our time space and we react accordingly. Still, the moon has one of the most fascinating landscapes in the universe and is now open for business.

Since they discovered huge quantities of water, vital to the subsistence of men on the moon, we can already book flights and rooms in the new Hilton.

It will take time for this to materialise, but it's all set.

Funny though. They've discovered water on the moon recently, but I knew this 20 years ago when I read

"Tintin: Explorers on the Moon."

The Russians paved the way in 1959 when their rocket landed. When Louis Armstrong became the first man who allegedly set foot on the moon. We are left to believe a lot of things about the moon. The moon has always been an excellent substitute for lassitude, jadedness and boredom.

related links

The moon

entry date: 07.02.00

38. "Y2K Showcase [February] is Upon Us"

Tonight, is the night.

We will finally get a

grip on the Y2K virus.

The venue is in London, apologies for being so self-centred, it's just because we happened to be based in London.

The address is Notre Dame Hall, Leicester Place, off Leicester Square, WC2.

18:00 for 18:30. No theme is the theme of the night.

Free champagne and a luscious cold buffet will be served.

See you there!

entry date: 08.02.00

39. "DavidBowie.com"

The opening page and main home page is a rather nondescript, gruesome yet intricate graphic with DB blurred in the middle on a white background.

We know after serious consideration that this is David Bowie's official site thanks to an elaborate timeline highlighting the different services offered by the stock-market whiz-kid.

Click here to join <u>BowieNet</u> the internet connection, here for members, here to view and buy David's work of art, here to go on, over there for, yes, he finally did it: The Bowie bank and apply for a credit card online with a luscious picture of David on the front.

One can access the links to an infinite amount of fan sites. There is an ingenious timeline to time warp the life of David over 30 years of successful career viewed through his 30 different album covers. One is also able to download samples of his music or stream it live and of course, buy it online.

One remarkable feature stem from the ability offered to recompose one of his songs and play it back with different instruments.

related links

<u>Bowie's official site</u>

<u>Our February Showcase</u>

entry date: 09.02.00

40. "The News Business"

<u>ITN (UK)</u>

<u>BBC (delayed news)</u>: came to our February showcase

SKY

CNN

Reuters : couldn't come to the February showcase

The Observer (UK): You're a competitor!

Euronews

The Times (UK) : they are still thinking about coming

Bloomberg

Cable NBC

The Guardian (UK) : "what's that?"

The Telegraph (UK) : came to our first showcase

The Evening Standard(UK) : a reporter came

The New York Times : sent their best wishes

The Los Angeles Times : "thanks but it's too far!"

The International Herald Tribune : someone came

The Independent (UK) : someone came

A tower of 'news'. Any takers?

entry date: 10.02.00

41. "Rock Culture"

Defines Rock music. Energetic music. Rebellious Art.

No pop rubbish.

entry date: 11.02.00

42. "Euphemism"

John and Mary, age 5 and 8. They both live in London.

- What's your euphemism?   [Mary]

- What's a euphemism?   [John]

- A substitute for thoughts.   [Mary]

- Mine's Mary for John.   [John]

- I'm your euphemism?   [Mary]

- It's easier that way.   [John]

When I get told off, I just say Mary did it!

entry date: 12.02.00

43. "Water"

related links:

Map of Universe

Time magazine Flash presentation of water pollution

Water and rivers resource site.

entry date: 13.02.00

44. "Lightning Strikes"

related links:

The day my life changed forever.

Refresh your PC software.

A FANTASTIC New York theatre company.

Survivors of electric shocks.

National Geographic.

CNEWS stories.

Photo gallery.

Infinite photo gallery.

Discovery channel news online.

A collection of lightning data.

Screensavers.

entry date: 14.02.00

45. "Beauty Book"

Join me.

entry date: 15.02.00

46. "Beauty Book"

Next,

entry date: 16.02.00

47. "Beauty Book"

Finally,

entry date: 17.02.00

48. "Elements of the Universe"

Images taken from the film Map of the Universe.

entry date: 18.02.00

49. "The Telephone"

Mary and John, age 5 and 8. They both live in London.

- Graham Bell invented the telephone.   [Mary]

- Rubbish! Erickson and Orange did.   [John]

- They weren't even there when he was alive.   [Mary]

- What 's got to do with it?   [John]

- Dad's Orange, so Orange invented it and it's a   [Mary]

phone all right.

JD

related links:

Erickson, Orange, Graham Bell.

entry date: 19.02.00

50. "The Belinograph"

Sending pictures over the phone line since 1910.

1897: Edouard Belin, a French engineer, began to experiment
with facsimile transmission. He then researched the history of

radio and the related media services of telegraphy, telephony, facsimile, television, photography and cinema.

The project will also develop an on-line resource centre based on the belinograph. Without a shadow of a doubt the direct ancestor of the internet.

My grand-mother used it in the 1920's to send images and moving images through the phone line.

Though, apparently for moving images it was a nightmare as it always took forever to reverse the process back into the moving pictures.

related links:

Belin. An historical timeline.

entry date: 20.02.00

51. "Andy Warhol"

related links:

Warhol museum.

Warhol home page.

Fans, forum and chat.

Warhol Arts.

entry date: 21.02.00

52. "The Negative of an Image"

Here

entry date: 22.02.00

53. "The Amiga"

"So, the World May Know," says the title.

Amiga announces plans to embrace Sun's Java technology as the software platform for forthcoming new Amiga products.

"Amiga is the home of a large number of the world's leading-edge multimedia developers, artists and users," so they keep saying.

Their web site is on our current list of the ugliest websites of the year. One of the most exciting links is the "retired Amiga products" displaying a blank page. We tried it a few times, from different machines but to no avail.

It is hard to find out who they are targeting.

Amiga seemed to have died in the nineties despite several promises of world domination.

related links:

Visit the Amiga site for more info.

Java developed by Sun.

entry date: 23.02.00

54. "Atari Baby"

The mega hit video game; "Pong" launched the electronic game industry in 1972. Atari, a new enterprise led by the legendary Nolan Bushnell, was the company that created and launched the "Pong" game.

In the 1980s Atari expanded into the home market with the Atari 2600 video console, selling tens of millions of games to home players.

As part of its strategy to deliver the best in electronic games, Hasbro Interactive acquired Atari and its games in 1998. Now Hasbro is reinventing Atari games for PC, video and Internet platforms, adding the latest graphics, audio and technology.

Atari was an altogether different breed. They were the first computer to display Cubase, the music software machine enabling the user to fit their sampling arrangement into a floppy. Hardly believable these days.

related links:

Review the history of the Atari. Peruse a fan's site.

entry date: 24.02.00

55. "Silicon Graphics"

related links:

FAQ's provided by Internet FAQ Consortium and Texas A&M University. Visit SGI online at Silicon UK.

entry date: 25.02.00

56. "Colour"

The colours (colours) of the spectrum.

entry date: 26.02.00

57. "Copyright, Patent and Registration"

Copyright does exist on the internet

entry date: 27.02.00

58. "Planet Earth"

There isn't much left of it.

The planet has been around, well, for almost 5000 years... In selfish human terms, that is. In earthling terms, a few million years and in Christian computing terms 2K. I can't remember being there at the beginning. I can remember how it all started. In the late eighties, everyone was displaying their green credentials to save the endangered planet. "Global warming" and "Recycling" were the norm!

Now the British government is spending millions in useless advertising campaigns on recycling and global warming, forgetting to provide the facilities and create the market.

The only recycling that has ever proven to be working is in the media... From ideas to back catalogues of film and music. Still, it is not too late for an earthling revival.

related links:

Greenpeace. Friends of the Earth.

Amnesty International. WWF. UNICEF.

RSPCA. National Geographic. NASA.

entry date: 28.02.00

59. "My Beauty Book"

Beauty

entry date: 29.02.00

60. "Programming

Basic. Text, number and one colour green. Very old.

Cobol. My first attempt in programming. It used to be a professional vocation in itself. A bit of an obsolete language.

Pascal (after the philosopher / mathematician), now Delphi.

Valid keywords in Pascal: Integer, Char, Record, Case, Real, If, While, With, Else.

// Program TWOQUOTES:

begin

  writeln('Hello there. I'm fine.')

end //

C and C++ have overridden the first three as graphics features badly needed to be included.

Mars

entry date: 01.03.00

61. "Programming"

<u>C</u>. First binary language tackling graphics in an acceptable format.

<u>C++</u>. Everything else seems to be based upon that.

<u>Visual Basic</u>. PC basics in visual design.

C++

```
class String {

    char *char_ptr;  // pointer to string contents

    int length;      // length of string in characters


public:

    // three different constructors

    String(char *text);    // constructor, existing string
```

String(int size = 80); // default empty string

String(String &Other_String);   // for assignment

              // from another object of this class

~String() {delete char_ptr;};   // inline destructor

int Get_len (void);

String operator+ (String &Arg);

void Show (void);

};

entry date: 02.03.00

62. "Programming (part 3)"

HTML, HyperText Mark-up Language.

Very simplistic even at its most technical.

HTML

<HTML>

<HEAD> <TITLE>The Title<TITLE> </HEAD>

<BODY BGCOLOR="#FFFFFF" TEXT="#000000">

  <FONT FACE="Arial" SIZE="2">

Everything else in here, within <B> type tags

and always closed with </B></FONT>

</BODY> </HTML>

DHTML, benefits mainly in Internet Explorer, though features such as Cascading Style Sheets work in Netscape.

Adding more substantial lay-out options.

DHTML

<STYLE SHEET="text/css"> BODY {

  background:white url(../title.gif) repeat-x;

} </STYLE>

entry date: 03.03.00

63. "Communication (part 1)"

Never travel without it. But when commuting in London is a legal inferno, I really start wondering about how easy it is for anyone to get away with anything. London's public transport can be hell at most hours.

Take the tube profits ridden to the core of their expensive advertising display on the walls to the back of the tickets for instance. When tremendous delays, crushes and overcrowding define the tube system they are still adamant: you are contemplating the 8th wonder of the world.

They hit the jackpot when they've introduced an on the spot £10 penalty to anyone travelling without a valid ticket on arrival. It happened to me. An underground gush of wind swallowed it. I thought I would have been saved thanks to my credit card receipt. How wrong I was.

I wrote a note to complain about this misfortune and sent it by recorded post. We're talking about six months ago! I'm still waiting for a refund despite several phone calls. JD

related links:

London Underground, currently in our list of Worst Websites.

entry date: 04.03.00

64. "Lonely Planet. Travel Guides"

For web monkeys and travel junkies. Search for a destination, anywhere in the world. All your travel problems. Lonely Planet (BBC owned) guides are a vital component for any exotic travel.

" Lonely Planet guides

are a vital component for any exotic travel. "

A typical guide will be: "Africa on a shoestring", discover Africa using this essential budget guide. UK: £17.99

US$29.95.

Featuring: 240 detailed maps up-to-date advice on visas, border crossings and staying healthy information on popular and safe travel routes.

Background on history, politics, culture and the environment heaps of good value accommodation listing comprehensive coverage of places to eat, from local eateries to Internet cafes useful sections on local and widely spoken languages. JD

related links:

Lonely Planet & Links to pictures, video and video sites.

Photo journalism and new media.

entry date: 05.03.00

65. "Communication"

To crown the finest P.R. ever, those underground people have announced Y2K as an 'es   ca

la

to

r-

free' year on the Victoria line.

This means that all passengers disabled or otherwise will have to tread along hither and thither to the best of their ability for the same overrated price.

This was <u>London Underground's supreme</u> commitment to an impressive multi million pounds investment in refurbishment. What no one could see is any sign of work taking place, thus inducing me to believe that it is both a fantastic P.R. coup and an electricity cost-saving exercise.

It's amazing how people can get away with anything! JD

related links:

<u>Still in our list of Worst Websites, London Underground.</u>

entry date: 06.03.00

66. "TV Culture (part 1)"

Defines devotion to slouching, dependence, easy life.

related links:

EastEnders BBC soap (worst crap ever)

entry date: 07.03.00

67. "TV Culture"

Trash and more trash.

related links:

TV gay guide.

The key to American soaps.

TV nonsense.

Court TV.

Culture shock.

entry date: 08.03.00

68. "Paris, Paris"

related links:

Paris Web, everything about Paris.

Fashion TV.

Paris, "The Best Of".

entry date: 09.03.00

69. "Mars, the Red Planet"

Forget about the Mars Bar and the third month of the year.

We're talking about planet Mars.

Mars was alive and well when the earth was still silent.

According to the legend, the Martians descended to earth to build the Sphinx. Recent scientific research demonstrates that the Sphinx couldn't have been erected by the Egyptians as it is now dated as far back as 5000 years BC, when human civilization had barely started.

Weird coincidences of life.

related links:

NASA

entry date: 10.03.00

70. "Advertising and Publicity"

Make it public.

Declare it.

entry date: 11.03.00

71. "P.R."

A <u>diplomatic</u> strategy

endorsing <u>publicity</u>,

<u>advertising</u> and

<u>propaganda</u>.

ME

entry date: 12.03.00

72. "Propaganda"

Inventing some nonsense to promote a concept.

The bigger, the more effective.

Hitler was the king of propaganda.

<u>Lady Thatcher</u> a Queen.

Who's the Y2K propagandist?

entry date: 13.03.00

73. "Virus"

Humans are the biggest creator of viruses.

One creates viruses by misusing one's computer.

One spreads a virus by adopting an unhealthy lifestyle.

Y2K is the virus that thrills.

related links:

Anti-virus news.

Hoax.

entry date: 14.03.00

74. "Virus (part 2)"

related links:

The anti-virus connection.

I love you virus. (updated link)

entry date: 15.03.00

75. "Virus"

Y2K rotates and cycles around.

entry date: 16.03.00

76. "Monopoly. The Game"

Beautifully rendered 3D animations.

Produced by: Hasbro Interactive.

Developed by: Westwood Studios.

Minimum Requirements:

CPU 486/33, 8MB of RAM, Windows 3.11 or 95, 2x CD-ROM, 13-27 MB hard-disk space, VGA video, SoundBoard (optional).

Meaning: strictly PC.

related links:

Visit Monopoly.com.

entry date: 17.03.00

77. "E-"

A lot of people seem to be rambling about the Emachine nonsense.

The more we go on about it, the less likely we will move on and the bubble may rise but will explode, sooner rather than later.

E- was hip years ago.

Now "commerce" and the "stock market" are prolonging the E-usage in an unhealthy fashion.

There is cause for concern.

entry date: 18.03.00

78. "Programming"

<u>JavaScript</u>. Adds interactivity to your <u>HTML</u> documents.

JavaScript

<HTML> <HEAD> <TITLE>Y2K</TITLE> </HEAD>

```
<BODY BGCOLOR="#FFFFFF">

<SCRIPT LANGUAGE="JavaScript">

for(i=2; i < 9; i++) {

document.write("Hello, Y"+ i +"K!");

delay(aThousandYears);

}


</SCRIPT>

</BODY>

</HTML>
```

Code like that above breeds Millennium Bugs.

related links:

Check out Live Software. Get your fresh JavaScripts here.

Netscape's developer area. JavaScript Builder.

A Web reference on the subject.

Microsoft might know something.

entry date: 19.03.00

79. "Programming"

<u>Lingo</u>. Language used by <u>Macromedia's Director</u>. For games and interactive presentations. "On mouse up, go to the frame".

<u>VRML</u>. Virtual Reality Mark-up Language. Used to design 3D environments. VRML files are made up of nodes.

VRML

```
Separator {

  Texture2 {

    filename "/textures/filename.jpg"

  } Cube {

    width  1

    depth  4

    height 9

  }

}
```

VRML was first thought up by Mark Pesece.

Gavin Bell of Silicon Graphics implemented it in 1994.

Join the WWW-VRML mailing list majordomo@wired.com with the message "subscribe, www-vrml, your email address."

Visit the VAG (VRML Advisory Group).

entry date: 20.03.00

80. "Programming"

AppleScript. For the Macintosh operating system.

AppleScript

//

on run tell "Apple" not to crash

//

Unix. Highly technical and therefore powerful operating system.

Developed at AT&T's Bell Labs in the late 1960s.

Based upon C, this language is much more than an operating system as it is truly a multitasking environment.

MS-DOS. PC nonsense operating system of a now bygone era.

Java. Sun Microsystems' language for all platforms.

Well that's how it should be, but Billy Gates has his own agenda.

J++. Microsoft Java.

entry date: 21.03.00

81. "Programming"

Oracle. My mate Tom can read the oracles on the palms of my hands. He can tell me my good fortune. That makes him an Oracle reader.

When the Eighties came with a bang with bad music, make-up and dresses for men, so did the programming language that resulted in the Teletext. Most of the world used Teletext, whilst the French stubbornly experienced the Minitel.

Minitel is a little computer with a number to type such as 3615 then the name of the site. The graphics were as appalling as in Teletext. They both live to this day, despite the Internet being available to Digital TV users. Oracle is more than just Teletext, and it has evolved into an integrated Internet language. (All gone now)

related links:

Take a trip to either Oracle or MiniTel.

entry date: 22.03.00

82. "Programming (part 8)"

1. Y symbol. The definition of the Map of the Universe.

2. Y- The Map of the Universe.

3. The Y-GREEK is an entity.

4. In France, a Greek symbol. In classical Greece the symbol of dreams.

5. Y-chromosome, male chromosome enhances the power of life. A sex chromosome occurring only in male cells.

6. Y, chemical symbol of Yttrium.

7. Y a vitamin, the chemical substance that brings everlasting life.

8. Y is the twenty-fifth letter of our alphabet.

9. Y in algebra it is the second unknown quantity.

10. Y in geometry it is the second coordinate.

11. Y-a Y-shaped thing, an arrangement of shapes in lines.

12. Y-Yeomanry.

13. Y- abbreviation of YEAR (S). Y=year(s)

14. Y- a prep. Meaning 'with, together', seen in nouns + adj.

15. Y- the twenty-third letter of the Roman alphabet, derived, as are also U and V, from Greek Upsilon y. It is used to represent a consonant sound as in year.

16. Y- Mediaeval numeral: Y=150, Y=150, 000

17. Y- Level, a type of engineers' level whose essential characteristic is the support of the telescope, namely Y-shaped tests in which it may be rotated, or reversed end-for-end.

18. Y-moth: any of the genesis of destructive noctuid moths with a silvery Y-shaped mark on the forewings.

19. Y- Track, a short track laid at night angles to a railway-line, connected with it by two switches resembling a Y, used in reversing engines.

20. Y-Alloy, an aluminium-base alloy of duralumin type, containing copper 4%, magnesium 1.5%, silicon 0.7%, nickel 2%, iron 0,6%, and titanium o, 2 %.

21. Y (ggdrasil)- in Scandinavian mythology, an ash-tree whose roots and branches join heaven, earth and hell.

22. Y (HVH)- with added vowels: Yehovah (Jehovah), the Hebrew name of God in the Old Testament; named in

Yahwistic the postulated author, or authors of parts of the Hexastich, which God is regularly called by this name.

(The Hebrew name of God in the Torah, as in the Old Testament is also Jehovah)

23. Y-fronts, men's or boys' briefs with Y-shaped seam at the front. From various origins. Knowing that the Y is also a male chromosome enhancing the power of life, it seems interesting also to note, that in the classical Greek education men from an early age had to cover their front parts with a cloth, clearly defining the symbol "Y" on it. In the Incas, it is also interesting to note that the same garment was de *rigueur*.

24. Expression: Yy-'Yat yt' for that, 'ye' for the.

25. Y- Symbol for admittance

26. Y- bar. A crystal bar cut in 2-sections, with its long direction parallel to Y. A piezoelectric plate cut from a quartz crystal in such a way that the plane of the plate is perpendicular to the Y-axe of the crystal.

27. Y- capacitor. A radio interference suppression capacitor intended for applications where failure of the capacitor could lead to danger of electric shock.

28. Y-circulator. A circulator consisting of 3 identical rectangular waveguides joined in a symmetrical Y-shaped configuration with a ferrite post or wedge at the centre. Power that enters any wave guide emerges from only one adjacent wave guide.

28. Y- The total ease of altering current flow at a given frequency and voltage. The reciprocal of impedance. A quantity, which in rectangular form is as useful for parallel circuitry as independence, is for series circuits. The resultant

of conductance and susceptance in parallel. The resultant of reciprocal resistance and reciprocal reactance in parallel.

29. Y-Admittance expressed in semen (S) or into (X-1) [x is the omega sign and the - is on a bit higher]

30. Y=|Y|=Y MAGNITUDE

31. Y=Phase angle of admittance [before y is the O with a bar across "th" symbol]

32. Y-POLAR

33. Y-RECT

34. Y-YEAR

35. Y -a. admittance

   -b. Young's modulus.

36. Y-box, WYE BOX

37. Y-defection. Vertical deflection of the spot on the screen of a cathode ray tube. (XDEFLECTION)

38. Y-diode. The decoding diode in each of the Y Ines of a memory matrix. (XDIODE)

39. Y-drive. The driving source of energy for the y lines of a computer memory matrix. (XDRIVE)

40. Y-gain. The gain of the vertical channel of an oscilloscope or X-Y recorder.

41. Y- intercept=the y coordinate of the point at which a time or plane intersects the y-axis.

42. Y-MODEM

43. Y-matched independence antenna (WYE ANTENNA)

44. Y-rectifier (WYE)

45. Y-potential (WYE)

46. Y-winding (WYE)

47. Y-sink. The circuit or device into which the Y-lines of a memory matrix feed. (XSINK)

48. Y-injunction. A waveguide whose longitudinal axes from ay.

49. Y-shear. A subsidiary fault in a shear zone parallel to the shear direction.

50. Y-command on the Macintosh computer to put a disk away (obsolete).

51. Y- plate, one of the two deflections electrodes that deflect the electron beam vertically in an electrostatic cathode-ray tube.

52. Y-factor. A noise measurement factor for specifying the noise figure of a receiver. It is based on known cold and hot reference temperatures.

53. Y-match. Also called a delta match. A method of connecting to an unbroken dipole. The transmission line is faced out and connected to the dipole at the point where the impedance is the same as that of the line.

54. Y-punch on a Hollerith punched card, a punch in the top row, two rows above the row zero.

55. Y-lever. The longest lever of a weighbridge to which the steelyard's rod is attached.

56. Y-signal.
1. A luminance transmission primary which is 1.5 to 4.2 MHz wide and equivalent to a monochrome signal. For colour pictures, it contributes the finest details and brightness information.
2. A signal transmitted in colour television containing brightness information. The signal produces a black and white picture on a standard monochrome receiver. In a colour picture, it supplies fine details and brightness information. It is made up of 0.30 red, 0.59 green, and 0.11 blue.

57. Y-Symbol of Tyrosine

58. Y-bus. A matrix which contains the admittance of each element in an electric power-system.

59. Y-parameters. The input and output admittances that are used to characterise a two-port device (network).

60. Y-connection. A three-phase source or load, which is connected such that the elements are connected in parallel and are thus, represented in a schematic diagram in a Y or star-shaped configuration.

61. Y-The digital luminance and colour difference signals in ITV-R601 coding.

62. The Y luminance signal is sampled at 13.5MHz and the two colours difference signals are sampled at 6.75 MHz co-sided with one of the luminance samples. (R is the digitised version of the analogue component (R-Y), likewise B is the digitised version of B-Y. Y is pure luminance information, whilst the two-colour difference signals together provide the colour information.

63. Y- (From CMYK) the third colour of the printing process, (Cyan, Magenta, Yellow and Black) where combined together brings a full colour processing. *Quadrichromy.*

64. Y- or IS, an ancient golf situated in the Southwest region of Zuyderzee in Amsterdam. Today, the region is nearly

completely dried. A little part of the Southeast is used as a port.

65. Y-2K the millennium bug.

related links:

Defining Y++.

entry date: 23.03.00

83. "As Nature Intended: Naturist and Pagan Traditions"

Naturism is a philosophy consisting of being in the nude in distant contact with other fellow human beings.

Paganism is the attribute of the non-believers in Christianity. From a Christian angle, that is.

In general terms, it is for all those who believe in natural laws or to some extent in Humanism, believing in the development of human beings.

Keywords:

Humanists,

Hedonists,

Druids,

Pagans,

Nature,

Friends of the Earth,

Naturist,

National Geographic,

Stonehenge,

Vegans,

Vegetarians.

Use any of the above keywords in the AltaVista window and discover thousands of related sites.

entry date: 24.03.00

84. "Programming"

Perl. Brings a different level of interactivity into your web pages.

Stored in a cgi-bin folder on the web server, and called by users from a HTML front-end.

Can perform functions such as database management,

automated email replies and form verification, so creating applications like shopping baskets, online games, chat boards, etc.

Perl

```perl
foreach $pair (@pairs) {

   ($name, $value) = split(/=/, $pair);

   $value =~ s/%([a-fA-F0-9][a-fA-F0-9])/pack("C", hex($1))/eg;

   $value =~ s/\0//g;

   $value =~ s///g;


if ($allow_html != 1) {

     $value =~ s/<([^>]| \n)*>//g;

   } else {

     unless ($name eq 'body') {  $value =~ s/<([^>]| \n)*>//g;  }

   }

}
```

related links:

Scripts and CGI programming search engine.

Free scripts. World of Perl. Library

entry date: 25.03.00

85. "Radio Search"

This unique search engine enables you to browse every radio related subject in the world.

StarSearch - The Internet's First Music Search Engine.

On April 13th, iEntry and 3 Stars Entertainment launched a new search engine specifically designed to locate streaming radio stations and other Internet music sites. Search over

70,000 hand-picked music listings at any StarSearch website.

entry date: 26.03.00

86. "Radio Search. Take Two"

related links:

wtak.com

newradiostar.com

wdrm.com

murphyinthemorning.com

entry date: 27.03.00

87. "iBook"

I've just received a new iMac Power Book, a little treasure. Faster in every step of the way and designed to suit all your design requirements. Mine is blue.

My colleague Tom is not impressed because he's so mad about his dedication to PCs. "Pentium this and that, processor this and that, everything is cheaper and better with a PC."

I thought that the war between Macs and PCs was over a long time ago. I suppose things aren't only restricted to Macs! OK: they were there first for imaging and video but they are different, they perform with a different mind.

Having a different mind could be even more fulfilling. It's like working with a different logic.

related links:

 subscribe to Apple News or purchase on-line

entry date: 28.03.00

88. "Sharp VL PD6H Digital ViewCam"

I was so desperate to get my hands-on Sharp's latest digital camcorder (VL-PD6H), that everyone is raving about, that I had to abuse my Mastercard to acquire it.

"Now, that for a

film-maker is an

absolute orgasm!"

For £1000 one gets a detachable LCD screen monitor, external microphone and the supreme 'arty farty' bonanza: to be able to shoot black and white images in total darkness.

Now, that for a film-maker is an absolute orgasm! (Allegedly)

related links:

visit Sharp.co.uk or view the specification

entry date: 29.03.00

89. "Macromedia.com"

This is the home site of the 'Wonderland' that is Director,

Flash, Fireworks, Dreamweaver and friends. Now owned by

Adobe whose owners believe that they own the planet; Planet Earth that is.

All these magical applications are now the industry standard for designing websites, multimedia presentations and interactive animations.

Check out our previous <u>Y2K Showcase</u>, we used <u>Director 7</u> on a PC to assemble this presentation.

related links:

<u>visit Macromedia.com or check out Site of the Day</u>

entry date: 30.03.00

90. "The Edge Gallery"

<u>The Edge Analogue and Digital Arts</u>.

Sorry, Mother

by

<u>Lola D'Arling</u>

Celebrating 10 years of awesome pictures, paintings and photography on the theme of 21st century dementia.

Aaaga

by

<u>Debbie Harry</u>

related links:

<u>Visit The Edge online.</u>

entry date: 31.03.00

91. "Get Connected (part 1)"

With the emergence of new media, a now already obsolete word amongst the nerdy community, this transient fashion of digital life paved out of gold is another fad that will become an integrated part of mainstream life, as we know it.

The route is simple: in the morning we switch on to Big Brother at work to look after us until dinner time and then, in the comfort of one's own home we strike again on e-business, e-chat, e-sex, e-TV, e-radio, e-go, e-tit, e-cock, e-this, e-that, e-nonsense.

Deprivation of life is no longer part of one's own vocabulary. E is synonymous with a journey of self-discovery.

No more scruples, frustration or agonising self-denial.

The poor programming of today's television is making one feel bored beyond redemption. Interactive TV only works thanks to the internet. Both combined together and the biggest E really transmutes into pure Interactivity. JD

April

entry date: 01.04.00

92. "Get Connected"

Soon it will be free to browse the universe ad nauseam. It's time for transportation in one's own bedroom. As BT (British Telecom) advertises it: How can we choose an internet service provider, when one is spoilt for choice between all these weird and wonderful names available?

How can we indeed? A name that we can trust like BT? And win a million pounds? Isn't it a little bit too good to be true? Or Demon (one of mine) with a name like that, need I say more?

And we need a few because one can be unavailable, too busy or simply that the network went down altogether. A name we all know is Virgin freshly brewed. Freeserve? For freedom of movement? American power with AOL free this and that. Freebies and goodies by the supermarket giant Tesco. What happens when Yahoo can't find this popular web address?

But they've promised you instant connection in their intensive advertising? Who will be here tomorrow? Who can tell? JD

related links:

Visit Jane online.

Usenet

Google is here to stay, whether I like it or not.

entry date: 02.04.00

93. "Get Connected"

The answer is simple: take a few.

This way, if one of these ISPs decides to collapse, you'll still have another one ready and bursting with energy. Who are these weird and wonderful ISPs? Are they an unknown entity skulking behind one's screen in a dark London bedroom approaching hard disk capacity, ready to detonate at any moment? Will you be that unfortunate victim who just lost all of their data in the fourth dimension?

In this age of stock, shares and internet boom, everything is speeding beyond belief and one has to trust one's own judgement. The answer is, as BT puts it: "a name that you can trust," whatever that means.

Still, all internet companies based in the UK are subject to strict rules of conduct and can be reported at any time if something drastic occurs, though, as always, the biggest and oldest is always the most trustworthy of all.

However, they also have a proven track record of poor customer service relations as opposed to the freshly brewed, eager to please. More help and guidance can be obtained from the <u>Consumer Association</u>. JD

entry date: 03.04.00

94. "Get Connected (Part 4)"

Finally, some of you devoted readers and nerdy fanatics may wonder what this review is in aid of? Well, let's face it, you're already reading these few lines therefore you're connected.

This is not merely about a connection seen whilst at college or when browsing at an internet cafe, a friend's place, the office or indeed one's bedroom, but by the confusion generated between all these "weird and wonderful names", eloquently put by BT, between the choice of a network breakdown and the orgasm reverberated by the new digital frontier without downtime, crashes and all the rest of it... JD

"...the orgasm reverberated by the new digital frontier..."

entry date: 04.04.00

95. "Nullsoft WinAmp"

If you are unable to live without music, then your life just keeps getting better by the day.

With the development of the <u>MP3</u> technology, a new chapter has opened up in the music industry. You can now store your whole music collection on a hard disk drive, and either play it from there or transfer tracks at will to a portable player.

The former is achieved by using a piece of software such as WinAmp (pictured right) to decode the audio files for real time, high quality playback.

WinAmp's features include: Equaliser, Playlist Editor, Visual Plug-Ins, Browser, 'Skin'-able, Streaming, CDDB, along with the usual play/shuffle/track controls, and loads of other features.

But the best thing by far is that it is now freeware!

So, what are you waiting for? Go get it! TN

related links:

download WinAmp, get some tunes.

entry date: 05.04.00

96. "IT-Opportunities.co.uk"

Thousands of jobs available every day in the IT sector, at IT-Opportunities.co.uk.

Just enter your area of expertise, location (and this can be anywhere in the world). A user-friendly solution to all IT job hunters.

related links:

find a position at IT-Opportunities

entry date: 06.04.00

97. "Watercolour C21"

How refreshing! How un-nerdy!

Organised by the Royal Watercolour (UK spelling) Society, Watercolour C21 is unlike most other watercolour painting competitions; there are no restrictions about size, subject matter or indeed age of artists.

The selection panel for Watercolour C21 consists of: Andrew Graham-Dixon, Chief Art Critic at <u>The Independent</u>; Eileen Hogan RWS, Emeritus Professor of the <u>London Institute</u>; and Sandy Nairne, Director of national programs at the <u>Tate</u> Gallery.

Prizes for the <u>Open</u>, which is supported by the international law firm <u>Freshfields</u>, amount to £10.000. Winning prizes and showing work in the exhibition at London's <u>Bankside</u> Gallery.

Hand-in days for work to be submitted to Watercolour C21 are Saturday 1 and Sunday 2 July. Artists are invited to send a SAE to Bankside Gallery, 48 Hopton Street, London SE1

9JH for an application form.

related links: no internet presence as yet

entry date: 07.04.00

98. "SlashDot"

News for Nerds. Stuff that matters.

Originally created in September of '97 by Rob "CmdrTaco" Malda, SlashDot is today owned by Andover.net. SlashDot is run primarily by Jeff "Hemos" Bates and Robin "Roblimo"

Miller. But the majority of the work is done by the tons of people who email stories...

News that no one cares or dares to publish. You can download some very interesting texture maps and 3D plug-ins.

They also have an incredible source of information about nanotechnology...

related links:

Go to SlashDot now!

entry date: 08.04.00

99. "Laurie Anderson"

The Grande Dame of multimedia strikes back with Moby Dick.

In a state-of-the-art production at the London Barbican, she will turn <u>Melville</u>'s masterpiece, "For we are all killers, on land and on sea, Bonaparte and sharks included," into a highly interactive multimedia opera.

At the <u>Barbican Theatre</u>

London EC1 on May 24th

Box office: 020 7638 8891

Photograph by

Frank Micelotta (Laurie Anderson)

related links:

<u>More info at LaurieAnderson.com,</u>

<u>and Barbican.</u>

entry date: 09.04.00

100. "The-Penis.com and The-Clitoris.com"

The first of which is a site dedicated to providing detailed information about the penis and male sexuality, as well as male sexual health, masculinity, and the joy of being a man!

All rendered in a funny, maybe naughty but tasteful compound.

Everything you need to know to really please your partner.

The other is a site that certainly deserves a mention. With many tasteful diagrammatic pictures of the clitoris. For men who lack knowledge of how to please their partner(s) or those who want to know more about the location and appearance of the clitoris, this is a "must".

They'll really thank you for taking the time to learn more! And these sites are both pretty extensive. JD

CAUTION: Although these sites provide an informative and humorous vision of female and male sexuality, we recommend that you must be of 16 years of age to enter, as they deal with adult topics. ED

related links:

venture to The-Penis.com, or The-Clitoris.com

entry date: 10.04.00

101. "BECK'S : futures"

A new generation of artists at the Institute of Contemporary Arts at the ICA, The Mall, London SW1.

Featuring Liz Arnold, Martin Boyce, Roderick Buchanan, Chad McCail, Lucy McKenzie, Stephen Murphy, Hayley

Newman, David Shrigley, Cathy Wilkes, Elizabeth Wright flying high in painting and sculpture to film, video and photography.

This exhibition aims at identifying and showcasing the most exciting new and emerging British artists.

date: 17th March - 17th May

time: Midday - 7.30pm

entry: £1.50 and £2.50 week-ends

box office: 020 7930 3647

tickets@ica.org.uk

Sponsored by Becks, the project marks the culmination of fifteen years of high-profile arts sponsorship and will offer the first glimpses of the future direction of visual arts in Britain.

Related links:

the exhibition site, sponsored by Becks

entry date: 11.04.00

102. "Paul Gambaccini"

Writer, broadcaster and one of Britain's finest and most exciting radio icons, delves into his most infinite self.

Sound, pictures and occasional Live Chat where you can ask

everything you always wanted to know about Paul and his life in nearly thirty years in broadcasting.

You can also email all your questions to Paul from this site.

related links:

personal site of Paul Gambaccini,

designed by Tom Norwood (2000).

entry date: 12.04.00

103. "Alta la Vista!" (Now: 2011: part of Yahoo)

Y2K Diary [12.04.00]

The world's oldest and greatest of search engines.

When some can offer only 35% of the world's resources, too busy concentrating on dealing with mortgages and credit cards like Yahoo or resembling a home-made search machine like Lycos, AltaVista offers to scan entries and even review some of them like a giant magazine.

"...the ultimate locus

to search for that

untraceable..."

Most academics and scholars will vouch that Altavista is the ultimate locus to search for that untraceable book or news item.

Make it your bookmark by bookmarking the Y2K showcase on your browser.

Related links:

find yourself with AltaVista

entry date: 13.04.00

104. "Free Speech Online Opposing Internet Censorship!"

Y2K Diary [13.04.00]

104. Free Speech Online Opposing Internet Censorship!

The EFF (Electronic Frontier Foundation) and other civil liberties groups ask that a blue ribbon be displayed to show support for the essential human right of free speech, a fundamental building block of free society, affirmed by the U.S. Bill of Rights in 1791, and by the U.N. Declaration of Human Rights in 1948.

Nevertheless, legislators and regulators in the US and around the world are intent on telling you what you and your children may read.

"Please help us teach the government that such a decision belongs in your hands, and those of every other Internet   user and parent."

The Blue Ribbon will be a way to raise awareness of online censorship and freedom issues, from locally to globally.

related links:

support Free Speech online

entry date: 14.04.00

105. "Snails"

Y2K Diary [14.04.00]

Snails are some of my favourite animals.

As I've written in my film Map of the Universe, coming soon to a cinema near you, that snails symbolise the long achievement of time.

According to a pagan legend, if you're very nice to them and look after them, they will return the favour. Though, I think this is also true of all our fellow brothers of the animal kingdom.

This site is about snails and some of its metaphors. Everything you were always dying to know about them.

Although the site is well documented and informative, there is very little about their sexuality. Not many people know that they do satisfy their own sexuality.

I might well research the subject one day and write a book about it. The site also has many links to other animal sites.

related links:

learn about snails

entry date: 15.04.00

106. "Scary Monsters and Super Creeps"

Y2K Diary [15.04.00]

In recent weeks a certain number of magazines and newspapers around Europe and America have reported scary stories about rats and mice. We thought we ought to find out more about it... In a town like London alone it is reported that the rat population is almost one billion, but who can really tell? A proper census would be rather difficult to conduct.

Edgar and Huxley of

SlapHog.com

A rat-tastic site for rat lovers with a selection of Rattie Links Galore to other sites, clubs and organisations and products.

- Latest information for those who still believe that we react like rats and that we can torture them, just for the sake of it.

National Anti-Vivisection Society

- Offering photos, screensavers, links and tips on how to care about your babies. Furry friends

- Not creepy, disgusting, plague-ridden vermin. Squeakies.

- Learn some facts and figures about a family member.

An academic description

entry date: 16.04.00

107. "Testing Your Thoughts"

Instructions

Tick on your answer, then count your points.

8 points for response A, 5 for B, 3 for C.

Questions

1) What would you do if on a cruise on the Pacific Ocean, travelling on your own, by a beautiful night you accidentally happen to fall over the deck straight into the ocean and you're left behind struggling in the water and no one noticed that you'd gone?
2) What would you do if you're stuck in the middle of the night, in a foreign town with no money and no credit cards?

3) What would you do after having won one million pounds on the lottery, having left your job as a result and spent all the money after only one month?

4) What would you do if suddenly a general power cut hit your house and deprived you of electricity knowing that it is due to last for another week?

Choose your answers then check your score.

Whatever you have scored, your answers do interest me.

Please send them to: jane@y2kdiary.com

Love and kisses,

Jane.

entry date: 17.04.00

108. "Keyword: Understatement"

Used everywhere from news, advertising slogans and most recently in the BBC's trashy soap Eastenders. Now, that's an understatement!

(Understate. Express in greatly or unduly restrained terms. Represent as being less than it actually is.)

Groucho wrote: "It's not like this hasn't happened before". A form of understatement, understating the obvious.

Quite an understatement "...The documents have received an

extra-ordinary level of review and are understood to be complete." Represent as being less than it actually is. A formal account of... Under-facts.

One won't freely find out more on the subject through the online Oxford Dictionary as it now has heavy licensing fees, etc.

State your understatement: understatement of the day, ridicule is nothing to be scared of, writing understatements, clueless was an understatement, broken is an understatement long is an understatement, talk about an understatement!

entry date: 18.04.00

109. "e-mania"

Channel 4 is Britain's fourth national TV network. State-owned and successfully run. It has a cable and satellite film network, FilmFour and is planning to launch a whole list of digital channels before the end of the year.

Channel 4 has always been the home of talent discovery of the most ingenious and ground breaking. Nevertheless,

Britain's networks like so many of their American and European counterparts have lacked true innovation. With only a few producing 21st century output such as truly interactive programs, with content diving into the e-fever.

Well this is about to change with the e-millionaire show!

"Have you got a fantastic idea for a website? We've got millions to invest! Be an investor capitalist."

The show will be launched in May and if it matches its partners such as the giant <u>Andersen Consulting</u> and newcomers <u>Resolve Media</u>, presenting here the extent of non-content, graphic-free and worthless colours with media <u>Mook</u> in a seamlessly bland and gruesome fashion, the show promises to be very ghastly indeed.

entry date: 19.04.00

110. "The Blair Witch Project"

"On 21st October 1994, Heather Donahue, Joshua Leonard and Michael Williams hiked into Maryland's Black Hills Forest to shoot a documentary film on a local legend, 'The Blair Witch.' They were never heard from again. One year later, their footage was found. 'The Blair Witch Project' is their legacy." The site opens on an old *grimoire*. One can flick through the pages and get more information on the film, but not enough to my liking.

The <u>QuickTime</u> movies might have been better rendered as <u>GIF</u> animations, with background noises and a screeching agonising sound that seems to loop forever and ever throughout the site. Very annoying.

I had to switch the sound off.

I saw the film when it came out, and I then described it as a very good documentary. I'm not saying here that a film site must have a trailer, one can only veer towards the excellent slide-show presentation stunningly demonstrated on its American sister site which is much better designed, more entertaining and interactive.

related links:

Compare the UK and US sites for yourself.

entry date: 20.04.00

111. "The Blair Witch Project"

As I have mentioned, the trailers are a bit mean. By definition, one could see everything within a trailer. Being mean with footage will only imply that there isn't much in the film, which is not quite true.

When the film first came out it was alleged that the phenomenal success was due to its net presence. Although the site had a strong fan club amongst college students, the marketing of the film did not happen overnight and not only through the web.

Web marketing enhances traditional media if the media is traditional, such was this motion picture. Strict web marketing works for web only media, by definition, as it is the nature of the exercise. Virtual versus non-virtual. The staggering amount of traditional marketing and promotion helped to enhance this success. The makers of this horror-documentary are Eduardo Sanchez & Daniel Myrick, two college chums. The film is out on VHS and DVD and is suitable for 15 years and above.

related links:

Compare the UK and US sites for yourself.

entry date: 21.04.00

112. "Do You Suck Your Thumb?"

I do! Unrelentingly and unashamedly. I'm 27! According to world's figures from the World Health organisation. 18% of us suck our thumbs, 10-12% appear to be women. According to Dr. Adam "Thumbsucking is the process of sucking on the thumb for oral gratification. It is a powerful need in infants, and is a normal activity with its peak occurrence at about age two."

"If thumbsucking continues past age 4, malocclusion of the teeth (abnormal contact between the teeth of the upper and lower jaw) may develop. Sucking is the chief source of pleasure for an infant. Studies have found that sucking is not associated with weight gain in premature infants and decreased crying."

Adam seems to believe that thumbsucking is unnatural and a health hazard in adults. Is Adam implying that he favours alcoholism, heroin and cocaine addiction and heavy smoking? That is unclear. Some people could find it offensive to see others sucking on a fag. For all the millions of adults' thumbsucking worldwide hiding their method of tension relief, there is a place on the net for you. Exchange ideas, views, experience on the subject and meet other fellow suckers.

related links:

ThumbSuckingAdults.com

entry date: 22.04.00

113. "Queer Art"

In the next Y2K Showcase we will attempt to define the meaning of 'The Queer, the Ugly and the Beautiful.' This may not necessarily mean what it is implying. Although there is some art around that does deserve a mention. One such a resource is Queer Art.

The website has been set-up as a non-profit, educational forum for the display and discussion of queer art and culture. Much has been suppressed, much has been lost due to neglect or censorship, and a great deal has simply been overlooked.

"... artistic identity is moulded by myriad factors, an amalgam of gender, racial, ethnic and sexual, to name a few. But we also know that honest artistic expression by the queer

community plays a role in combating homophobia and advancing the principles of intellectual integrity."

This quintessential resource library must be on every artist and art lover's bookmarks alongside <u>The Tate</u> and the <u>Louvres</u>, for queers and non-queers a-like.

Although this is a traditional art gallery, it also dives into the interactive with infinite sensitivity.

related links:

<u>Queer-Arts.org for your perusal.</u>

entry date: 23.04.00

114. "Snoring"

A loud breathing during sleep, perhaps there is more to it.

According to Snoring-help.com 45% of adults snore at least occasionally. 25% are habitual snorers. Snoring is often related to physical obstructive breathing during sleep.

Not so many people know that it is a respiratory impediment that could lead to many complications. There is a <u>British Snoring</u> and <u>Sleep Apnea Association</u> but there is very little on-line help. Many sites are trying to plug their wonderful pills and expensive special treatment clinic, when the answer is often nearer than that.

The first answer would be to become aware of this state, research the subject and ask your chemist or your naturopath for an herbal treatment. Very often it only needs a little treatment.

Snoring is often associated with lifestyle, lack of exercise, personal problems, and sinus infection. If the symptoms do persist or if after a thorough research you find that you do resemble the case of someone with deep breathing problems and may need further help, then call your GP.

related links:

A medical compound neatly concocted by Doctor Yahoo

entry date: 24.04.00

115. "The Ugly (part 1)"

As I have mentioned before, the theme for the next Y2K Showcase, on the 28th of April, is "The Queer, the Ugly and the Beautiful" and this may not necessarily mean what it is implying.

HappyDrunks.com is happy to say that the internet is full of ugly people and presents some of the ugliest in their "Damn You're Ugly Award" and the content we are warned is for a mature audience.

The ugly people's site displays their own embarrassing pictures as well as a chart of Britain with all the different regional accents. These webmasters are all chasing their very own ugliness.

When a site displays the site "under construction" it is also a form of ugliness.

Better have no website than this mention, better have one image without the mention at all.

related links:

Find the Ugly People.

entry date: 25.04.00

116. "The Ugly"

We are still dealing with "The Queer, the Ugly and the Beautiful", the theme of the next Y2K Showcase on the 28th of April. We talk, see and paint them as if there were a work of Art. But they are an art form in their own right.

A list of ugly recommended web pages:

Butt-ugly Web Design

World of Bad Taste, Bad Design and Kitsch

It's time to K B /   Is This Annoying

No One Knows Who Owns This Page

Stev0's (Hideously Netscape "Enhanced") Home Page

One of the small wonders of modern technology

Surrender to Netscape!

Steve's Totally Obnoxious Web Page

I'm Sorry   /   Biff's Home Page   /   Annoying U

Alexandre Petit-Bianco   /   Argyroneta

Web Page Demolition Inc.

Bad Use of Bandwidth

Web Pages That Suck (This page sucks a bit too :o)

The Good and the Bad

The Loons

Alex's Home page

entry date: 26.04.00

117. "Who wants to be a Millionaire?"

Are we obsessed with this word? Everyone seems so desperate to get rich, and right now. Is it merely an act of extreme desperation or the dire extent of our achievement? There are a myriad of sites promising you the world, just as long as you have a credit card. An overwhelming amount of game shows will ensure your entrance to Midas' Kingdom. One can also follow the trend and become a .com millionaire. Going on the stock market could be a rough path to follow. Losing nearly a third of its value with LastMinute.com is not the most advisable path to venture into.

It is important to remember that over 80% of existing Internet firms will dissolve within the next year without making a single penny in profit. A lot of people will lose money in the process, but some will be agile enough to make a quick get-away in the nick of time with most of the proceeds. They will be the real millionaires. There is no real recipe. Game shows, .com, the lottery or simply that bright idea that will change the world?

related links:

TV's most celebrated, everything is in the logo :oP

Make a quick million, slap-dash leisure at the last minute.

entry date: 27.04.00

118. "SONIC BOOM: The Art of Sound"

I've just returned from the PR launch. The exhibition opens today and runs until 18th June. I couldn't wait to place this entry. As a musician and multimedia artist, I should know better and play with words as eloquently as this exhibition inspires. But it's not easy.

The Art of Sound includes over 25 artists including Brian Eno, Scanner, John Oswald to name but a few. They've all joined forces in an attempt to capture the sound of our digital era and recompose its message within an erratic, demented, freaky and technologically profane environment.

The fine use of the space provided does add to the grandiloquence of the atmosphere. I'm literally bewildered.

The place was far too crowded to even glimpse further. I'll have to return and scrutinise every piece of installation, projection, sound and get involved, get stimulated, get pictured and shiver to every bit of noise, one can indulge to capacity.

Talks and live performances will take place in other venues.

related links:

see The Hayward Gallery site for more info

entry date: 28.04.00

119. "Blue (part 1)"

Colo(u)rs. Variation on Blue.

Opening the mind.

Deconstructing the message.

Re-enacting values.

Claiming the present.

Moving on. Blueprint.

entry date: 29.04.00

120. "What's Wap?"

Prudential, the pension company and Vodafone, the mobile phone company have announced a new financial service for mobile phone users. Using a <u>WAP</u>-enabled technology, any mobile phone can access the services via the UK's only WAP directory.

Prudential will act as a consultant for its range of financial services, ranging from pensions, insurance, services and loans.

WAP-Wireless Application Protocol. According to the Financial Times, 90% of new mobile phones will be WAP-enabled by December 2000.

Wap is an easy and secure access to relevant Internet/intranet information and other services through mobile phones, pagers, or other wireless devices.

related links:

<u>the WAP forum.</u> wap.com.sg includes downloads, discussion, solutions, and more. Cover concepts of wireless applications, the WAP, and its associated architecture. The Independent Wap. Wap Warp, A Warp search engine. More information on <u>Prudential</u> and <u>Vodafone</u>. Also, The <u>Financial Times</u> can shed a little light.

entry date: 30.04.00

121. "Fluorescence"

The property of absorbing light and diffusing it simultaneously.

This reflection could be visible or invisible as with x-rays, ultraviolet light and cathode rays.

This is the front cover of my ill-fated album of 1997: **LoudMouth**.

May

entry date: 01.05.00

122. "Blue"

entry date: 02.05.00

123. "Nano World"

In my own secret den in downtown London, Hoxton N1, the heart of the loonyland (left wing/Stalinist snob what the French are calling "gauche caviar") expat from uptown Islington vehemently trying to compete with uptown Soho, (in the media world, one understands) I often wondered how the whole world would look if narrowed to an infinitesimal quantity, a microscopically imperceptible Lilliputian minuscule entity.

Almost invisible.

Accessing this world by scanning a bar code containing the data hitherto mentioned.

Planet earth, that is. Enter the nano world in all its divine technology. Within a nano second (one thousand-millionth of a second) one could time warp in and out memory lane and "be" here, there and everywhere... The Technology of the 21st Century. JD

related links:

Provides a brief introduction to the core concepts of

molecular nanotechnology, a fantastic magazine devoted to the subject, some forum and chat.

We have reviewed Slashdot magazine before, they have an incredible amount of nanotechnology stuff.

entry date: 03.05.00

124. "Rocky Horror"

We have been so busy putting the new features into the Y2K Showcase, Y2K Forum, Y2K TV, Web live, this and that etc., that we've almost forgotten that we have entered into the merry month of May! And Mayday in all its significance. Apologies.

In the revival season, I'm forced to review a musical that I tried to forget. Richard O'Brian's "The Rocky Horror Picture Show."

Scream through the time warp again and this time, it is not in a grotty West End venue but The Hackney Empire. It sounds already like its groundbreaking heyday of '74.

It's alive and interactive.

Open your umbrella when it rains; stand up when you must, lift your leg up when you can. The sweet transsexual from Transylvania is back in a sumptuous-edgy presentation.

And remember the old post-punk new-age adage: "Don't dream it, be it!" You might wish to see the film first or hear the CD, as you'll be requested to perform in due course! JD

related links:

The Hackney Empire.

Twentieth Century Fox - the official site.

Yahoo film fact sheet. A mad site. Learn the dance.

entry date: 04.05.00

125. "Chess (part 1)"

Chess is a game played on a square board of 64 black and white squares with 32 pieces of different values.

16 men each (apparently, but there is a Queen as well) and "Checkmate" signals the winner of a game.

The game is almost emphatically subliminal and metaphysical. For instance, a knight (horse) can only move within a definite pattern (L) clearly outlining a marine's cross or a celestial chart. It's almost as if somehow, there was a hidden number skulking behind each shape. As if a chess game and everything in it was a gigantic map to follow.

An intrinsic map of the universe.

related links:

Tomorrow is another day.

entry date: 05.05.00

126. "Chess (part 2)"

The King of chess

Online play

Yahoo chess online

Java based game for beginners and advanced

Chess Lab, Java interface to chess games online

JavaScript enabled incarnation

Important dates in chess history

Questions about chess

Macintosh chess

Books about chess

Classic problems with solutions

The London Chess Centre, download, tips and online magazine

entry date: 06.05.00

127. "The Element of Style"

"Alea, jacta, est". Never overload a text with pretentious jargon, that no one, certainly not the author will even remotely comprehend. "I, I, I", "overly", "so meaningful". Web pages are full of 'them'.

"Under Construction" syndrome seems to be popular.

Defined as ugly in our current showcase, it is sometimes unavoidable. Though, when it is there for weeks on end and advertised at the end of an article in a daily newspaper, it becomes a GAG. A gag could be a statement, as long as we are aware of this. Achieving style in grace of attitude will certainly not pop up like a jack in a box.

It comes by acknowledging one's self, in one's own beauty, one's ugliness and one's queerness.

I'm certainly still after it. I'm "Under Construction".

<u>The Element of Style</u>" is also a cult book in writing by Strunk and White published by Allyn and Bacon.

". sell your virginity for nothing.com" is also very popular.

The infamous "dot" so dear to Absolut Vodka in the Eighties, became a de facto component of life in the nineties with ".com" and another definite must before anything in the Y2K years.

Not to mention stuck in the middle "easy.everything.com"

entry date: 07.05.00

128. "How Do We Do It? (part 1)"

entry date: 08.05.00

129. "How Do We Do It? (part 2)"

I've done it all before. Did it and done it. It does take time.

Doing, making, creating, building, bestow, perform, play, produce, carry out, produce, complete, achieve, acceptable, suit, transform, progress, process, deliver, provide, accomplish, act, execute, determine, engage, manage, direct, fulfil.

How do we do it? Simple!

"Do it, be it, achieve it and deliver it."

In part 1, we presented a movie defining the indecision, by producing a computer-generated fragment of a brain currently speculating on the how, who and precise why of this location.

entry date: 09.05.00

130. "Fluorescence"

radiance

elegance

eminence

effulgence

brilliance

glitterance

resplendence

luminescence

incandescence

related links:

Electric LadyLand is apparently the very first museum of fluorescent art using all kinds of fluorescent minerals.

entry date: 10.05.00

131. "Where Are We?"

I have no idea where we are.

entry date: 11.05.00

132. "Where Are We?"

Why is London so trendy?

Near Canary Wharf the asthma levels among children are twice the national average. US health studies show that soot particles known as PM10's kill 2000 people prematurely every year in cities like London, from heart attacks and respiratory problems. Sometimes the level goes as high as 140 to even 150 parts per billion.

SIX DEADLY TOXINS

An over-the-average cloud hanging over London is made-up of a deadly combination of nitrogen dioxide and the tiny particles of soot and dust PM10s. The main source of both pollutants is London's traffic, with industry contributing a tiny amount.

The pollutants have become trapped in the Thames basin by the current cold, windless weather conditions. There are six main pollutants caused by traffic emissions.

related links:

This is London, and London rats

entry date: 12.05.00

133. "Where Are We?"

Why is London so trendy?

There are six main pollutants caused by traffic emissions.

BENZENE: No safe level.

Causes cancer and poses a long-term risk of leukaemia.

BUTADIENE: No safe level.

Linked with cancers of the bone marrow and lymphomas.

NITROGEN DIOXIDE:

Increases risk of lung damage and respiratory infection in children.

OZONE:

Impairs lung function and increases sensitivity to allergens.

PM10s:

Tiny particles deposited in the lungs linked to heart and

respiratory disease and may be responsible for thousands of

deaths of vulnerable groups.

The worst British smog took place in December 1952 and lasted a week. It killed an estimated 4.000 through heart and lung disease. Coal burnt in homes and factories was then the main cause.

related links:

The Tate Gallery might cheer you up!

entry date: 13.05.00

134. "Vaudeville 2K"

Hydra presents: Vaudeville 2K on June 1st 2000.

As a grand gesture for the millennium, hydra is presenting a

brand new event!

In the gorgeous setting of The Old Brick Lane Music Hall (now sited in Curtain Road) we will be presenting a showcase of Performance and New Media work. Featuring 12 different performances, this one-off event is also a celebration of the Music Hall and its influence on contemporary work.

Live Art @ the Music Hall,

134-143 Curtain Road London EC2 3AR

Doors open at 7.45pm, the show starts

at 8.30pm and ends at 11.30pm.

Entry £8 / £5

07879 445229

Nearest Tube: Old Street

The venue is wheelchair / fully accessible

more info: hydra_liveart@hotmail.com

This unique event is made possible by the National Lottery

and supported by Coca-Cola

entry date: 14.05.00

135. "The Forum Is Open"

Do suckers have all the Fun?

Forum

Am I wrong in thinking that the poor morality of pricks
renders sex obsolete?

Forum

Lesbianism has become a party to which the world, especially
the male half, must be invited if it is to be deemed acceptable.

Forum

The rest of the story need not be taken in action, and indeed would hardly need telling if my imagination were not so cribbed by the sheer lack of objectivity and lazy care for my demented surrounding on the ready to wear slap-dash cocky bitches and pansies in which decadence keeps its toll of natural disasters.

Forum

entry date: 15.05.00

136. "What a Palaver!"

We've received, to date, 54 alarmed surfers regarding the three entries we did on the pollution in London.

It's true. It's all true.

I'm still adamant that London's pollution problems need to be addressed. A mainstream London that is.

I've no solution to it. Megacities are the dilemma of the 21st century. Only within a definite compound can we start to tackle the problem. This compound is awareness.

We have to learn to live with it. The more we eat and produce, the more consumed our environment will become. Fashion and trends have a habit of adapting to every situation, pollution included.

Breathing clean air will be London air and breathing the

country air will be like breathing London.

Isn't it great?

entry date: 16.05.00

137. "Redefine the Meaning of the"

What's really odd is after all these years there are still millions of media companies that have dramatically failed to even begin to comprehend how the web works.

A stagnant web site is one thing, poor information is another. Another what? One may ask. Just another lack of comprehension about what the Internet entails.

The net moves and moves very fast. To be efficient a site should not be merely a still poster, but a representation in another dimension and therefore has to be tackled accordingly.

Within the web amongst the millions of magazines, newsletters, search engines and other programs on offer. Its content should ideally be constantly updated.

The more interactive and accessible the web site is, the more hits it will generate. It is a different world, a virtual world, and must be approached with this in mind.

Its significance and infinite target audience has yet to feature in the agenda of many.

related links:

Log-on to the **Y2K Forum** and deepen the debate

entry date: 17.05.00

138. "Redefine the Meaning of the"

The "this is me and my picture" syndrome floating in cyberspace for years on end is sadly still the norm adopted by a lot of media companies.

Remember that in the last two years the web has taken 40% of the share audience from traditional media, TV and newspapers included. The Y2K Showcase is, modesty set aside, the living proof. Although we're also targeting the non-virtual media for marketing and hold showcases for a

back-up, the bulk of our effort has been concentrated on the web. Even with our average of 24000 hits a week, we haven't reached global status just yet. But it's significant. We will improve this score during the summer when everyone is supposedly sunbathing.

During the whole summer, starting in June we will dive in water, discover marine life, broadcast live underwater footage, mountain surf and all the things allegedly less Arty. Our web marketing will increase, but our non-virtual marketing will decrease.

This is the nature of virtual reality.

related links:

Log-on to the **Y2K Forum** and deepen the debate

entry date: 18.05.00

139. "Hahabonk.com"

Hahabonk.com (now defunct, they didn't last very long) is Europe's first web-based comedy channel and the world's first true cross-media comedy brand. Launched on April fool's day 2000, hahabonk showcases a brand of humour that is bold and irreverent.

Featuring content from the likes of Perrier award winning duo Ben 'n' Arn and Mackenzie Crook (11 O'clock Show) hahabonk offers users animations and short films from hot new and established sketch writers.

These shows also exist in the real world as hahabonk acts appear live at comedy clubs and stand up venues across the country. As well as showcasing new talent, they feature live performances from big name acts. Hahabonk will quickly spread to other mediums offering SMS and WAP services such as satirical news, show up-dates and games to mobile phone users. The impressive gamut delivered within the eloquent Flash presentation sparkles by its user-friendliness paves the way to its elaborate entertaining content.

Produced by: Empty Space (Now: defunct)

entry date: 19.05.00

140. "Y2K Showcase"

" The Queer, the Ugly and the Beautiful "

Friday 19th May 2000 between 19:30 and 22:00

upstairs at The Intrepid Fox

97-99 Wardour Street

London W1

Entry is Free!

entry date: 20.05.00

141. "Y2K Showcase"

The Y2K Showcase: "The Queer, the Ugly and the Beautiful" was fan-t-as-tic.

The showcase was a presentation of the web site. Announced for 7pm, a lot came at 8pm and a lot more at 9pm.

So, the " Queer " was a reference to the area in Soho, the " Ugly " was the choice of venue, the worst in the west end, and the " Beautiful " was the myth attached to the West End.

Equally, the theme was inspired by the world of media.

The next showcase is on the 30th of June and will be in Hoxton. An expanded team will organise the show...

Performance artists and short films are on the menu.

The whole show will be streamed on this site.

Watch this space for all the latest...

entry date: 21.05.00

142. "Of Feet and People"

There are literally thousands of websites dealing with feet.

It seems that the devotion to a barefoot goes beyond art as it becomes a lifestyle, a health frenzy, a religious devotion and a sexual fantasy.

related links:

Post messages about your feet

The naturists' point of view

Sample of questions and answers

A gallery of feet

Issues on health and safety

entry date: 22.05.00

143. "Suckers"

related links:

Dark sucker theory,

Incredible suckers; Cephalopods, cuttlefish to vampire squid

entry date: 23.05.00

144. "Baby Boom"

In a welter of PR exercise, the British Prime Minister successfully managed to deliver a baby through his wife Cherie, of course, on the eve of family week. Such timing couldn't be more appropriate for a politically troubled Mr. Blair.

But it's true. It's all true. There is a baby boom in the year Y2K.

With an overpopulated planet on the brink of explosion, it is ambiguous to commend the noble virtue of family life. Though, when it happens and it works, it's beautiful. One cannot help thinking about the PR exercise of some of the baby makers' machines.

Iman and David Bowie have announced their lovely one for August, thereby cleverly grappling the headlines. Well, why not? I just hope that all of them know what it entails and involves. A child is for life, not just for Christmas, not until they are beaten up and, in an age, to sleep rough in the streets.

Related links:

Childline UK,

NSPCC National Society for the Prevention of Cruelty to Children,

Centrepoint aims to ensure that no young person is put at risk because they do not have a safe place to stay.

entry date: 24.05.00

145. "Dolphins"

In their very own way, dolphins seem to be free and they try to communicate this to us humans.

If we could only listen, our lives would be far better as a result.

related links:

This is a beautiful resource site, in the world of dolphins, with images, facts and links to other dolphin sites.

entry date: 25.05.00

146. "Snow Me in the Summer"

Skiing is not thought to be a summery activity. Not many of us choose to ski in the middle of the summer. But there is snow and plenty of it and it's the most exhilarating experience ever. For this one needs a glacier located nearby a lake on a much lower altitude.

The program is simple; 9am On *telepherique* en route to the glacier. 9.30am Ski, ski and more ski until noon. Miles and miles of landscape and no one to be seen. 1pm Dive into the most translucent blue and warm water ever under a sizzling sun.

There are a few glaciers worth exploring this summer.

Most of them are in the Alps. Enjoy!

More details on where to find them: Summer Ski.

Picture taken from the film:

Map of the Universe

related links:

More exhilarating ski: Rapture TV available on the web, on cable and satellite in the UK.

entry date: 26.05.00

147. "Bored?"

Yesterday, a friend told me how bored he was.

I reacted violently. I was shocked.

How can you be bored?

You've obviously never seen the Y2K Showcase.

What about the thousands and millions of links that we have?

Boredom is assimilated with laziness. An extreme side of jadedness.

If you're still bored after reading these lines, or even if you're not, go to DullMen.com. They say: "We were delighted when we heard we've been chosen as the third most boring web site in the U.K."

The Boring Institute could certainly win our ugliest site of the year contest. This site left me somewhat flabbergasted.

The Lazy Lab will calculate the level of your boredom being equal to that of laziness.

entry date: 27.05.00

148. "In Life There Are Pigeons And Pigeons"

In London, depending on where you are, the pigeons will

come in all sizes, shape and colour. For instance: in Trafalgar Square, they are filthy, weak, crippled with broken wings. Given the impression that they are some refugees from a beach where gallons of oil leaked from a tanker.

Not so far, Neal's Yard in the centre of Covent Garden. This is the health food freak area. From organic beauty to natural healing. The pigeons there are comparatively healthy and happy, though they are orange, yellow, blue, pink and purple. No one has ever admitted to painting them that way, arguing that their colour was due to a healthy organic upbringing.

In the centre of Islington, the pigeons are healthy and overstuffed to capacity. Some can't even fly anymore, unable to drag their potbelly along. Interestingly enough, on nearby Upper Street in the heartland of restaurant society, pigeon seems to feature on some of the menus. Very strange!

related links:

Big Pigeon was established in March 1998.

A non-profit, artist run site promoting thoughtful, in-depth investigations and attempts to move contemporary art beyond cynicism. Includes an exhibition and forum.

entry date: 28.05.00

149. "Hands Off the Internet"

"The Internet is a bastion of free speech

and an endless canvas of possibilities."

"It's also prime real estate for government regulation."

"A war is being waged over the Internet and how you as a consumer will access it. The battle lines are drawn and you have to decide which side you're on. The side that limits or the side that innovates."

It's true that the future is direly uncertain.

Some say that 0ver 75% of websites will not be there tomorrow. The same rumours say that the web will mainly be accessible through the TV or the mobile phone and will therefore be strictly regulated.

Do we need regulation or guidance?

related links:

Hands Off the Internet.

entry date: 29.05.00

150. "Memory"

One often loses one's own memory.

It happens.

Intoxicating substances can seriously adumbrate the pictures in the mind.

Loss or fading memory is, contrary to popular belief, not an ageing problem. Some elderly can have a far greater memory than a 20-year-old. Memory like some RAM (Random-Access-Memory) needs to be serviced, maintained and upgraded.

70% of the world's population does not use their memory efficiently, whilst 65% do not seem to be using it at all! We either rely on tools or people in the vicinity to refresh it.

related links:

False memory myths in sexual abuse cases.

Stop the therapy syndrome for recovering memory.

An academic point of view with links. Resource centre on the subject. Mind Tools learning mnemonics techniques.

The Art of memory, a small intriguing feature.

Games and Secrets for using and enhancing memory.

entry date: 30.05.00

151. "June"

June is just 2 days away.

The summer will barge in with a bang. Our new look revamped website will shine and three new features will be revealed.

related links:

The summer solstice, and a directory of the summer solstice.

The most annoying music ever comes with the package.

Maybe not.

entry date: 31.05.00

152. "Dazed But Not Confused"

I'm somewhat dazed but not totally confused.

A touch of the flu, I expect.

Overworked.

Consumed.

Jaded.

Dizzied.

related links:

Smile

Dazed and Confused

June

entry date: 01.06.00

153. "Where is Everybody?"

There are only three solutions in the 21st century.

1) Home surfing.

2) Working out (Whatever that means).

3) On holiday.

The latter requires an experienced guide for that unusual travel adventure such as flying a jet fighter at 70,000 feet, diving on shipwrecks, riding Route 66 on a Harley, walking the South Pole or joining the waiting list for the moon trip promised for the year 2005.

One needs to be able to search a location, anywhere and then an occupation. Unless of course, one would prefer to dive further in the emptiness of a pristine white world devoid of all meaning, noise and contradiction.

related links:

Where will we go?

entry date: 02.06.00

154. "Where Are We Going?"

Some people have no sense of orientation whatsoever.

For all I know I could be sitting in the Northern Hemisphere, when actually this could be somewhere up East.

I always carry my street map with me, though I tend to lose it everywhere and it is becoming very expensive to buy one, every time I go places.

It's a common mistake. With all the lost guides in the world, there must be a huge wealth of street maps somewhere.

related links:

With StreetMap.co.uk London should hold no secrets.

Give MultiMap a postcode and Great Britain is your Oyster!

The whole world at your finger-tips with MapQuest.

entry date: 03.06.00

155. "Dante."

In Dante's Divine Comedy the stages of Inferno go through different steps…

entry date: 04.06.00

156. "South Park and the Simpsons"

Whilst South Park makes one feel bored beyond redemption as a direct result of over watching, the Simpsons is still enjoyable.

The first strikes in rude language and the second is reminiscent of my rebellious childhood. I can't help thinking that there are gruesome similarities between the two.

But I wouldn't know how to start pinpointing the many metaphors and discrepancies.

Both gave me more than my fair share of feel-goodness. So there!

related links:

The official South Park site (heavy to download), too many unnecessary items for my liking, more about the production company than South Park. South Park with the Macromedia makeover.

And finally, the pretty nondescript Simpsons site.

entry date: 05.06.00

157. "Jesus Christ"

If Jesus were alive today, he would undoubtedly be proud of

his omnipresent net appearances.

Jesus was allegedly vegetarian, Jewish, bisexual and anarchist.

That makes me somewhat even with him on the vegetarian and Jewish blood bit. Though, I'm far from being one of those going on about who's who and what's what. Perish the thought.

Still, he did deserve a mention and he got himself a mention.

Thundering Typhoons!

related links:

Jesus was a vegetarian, and did the Jesus dance.

Other silly-dance sites: the original Hamster dance or the Armadillo dance.

entry date: 06.06.00

158. "Naturist"

Of course, the same amount of web pages is clogging the network and yet this is another part of society completely ignored.

I wouldn't take my kit off in public for anything less than a million dollars, then again it is not a contest but a lifestyle and a philosophy. Apparently, running around naked in public is extremely healthy and good fun.

I'm not convinced but, as they say, can 30 million streakers be wrong?

related links:

The sport of streaking is celebrated here.

Hall of shame, some moralists seem to think that naturists are a bunch of old perverts. Then again, their site could be seen as equally doubtful, the writing is extremely aggressive.

entry date: 07.06.00

159. "The MP3 Saga (part 1)"

Edgar Bronfman Jr., chief executive of Seagram, the owner of Universal (Polygram, Polydor, Island, AM etc.) the biggest record label in the world, recently chucked in some dark threatening menace over the Internet.

"The web will crack, crumble and collapse if the constant ripping off of our music catalogue continues."

He's talking gobbledygook and he is responsible for owing money to thousands of artists who've been ripped off and myself included.

MP3 download is not a crime but a serious freedom of creativity and a thorough break on all Mighties still overcharging the price of music and not even redistributing the royalties to some of their artists. Even David Bowie, Stock

Market spinner and Net guru got the right approach. Offering to chuck every new album over the Internet for a limited amount of time.

Follow the debate on the Forum. Ends tomorrow (?).

related links:

The Y2K Forum for whole-hearted debate.

entry date: 08.06.00

160. "The MP3 Saga (part 2)"

People will still buy the real thing: the logo, the pictures, the video, the extras etc. Of course, it's much easier for him to operate this way because he owns his back catalogue.

Paul McCartney is pursuing all the companies and teenagers downloading his music. So sad. He obviously has nothing better to do. From the king of anti-establishment music. First you tell people to rebel, then return to feeding your bank account. Make your mind up!

MP3 is all about enhancing music. Some tracks should be made freely available on the web. Music will never survive in its current form. If Edgar Bronfman and Paul McCartney persist in their thirst for money they will soon face a herd of lawsuits from people in music who have been ripped off...by them.

The anger is growing.

The debate is open.

Log on to the forum.

related links:

Follow the debate on the **Y2K Forum**.

entry date: 09.06.00

161. "Buying MP3 (part 3)"

I'm not trying to fuel the MP3 debate. Whether you are downloading pirated songs or samples, good MP3 licensed music without a scratch can also be purchased online. Instead of branding totalitarian slogans, the peoples I then mentioned in the previous two entries should reconsider what they are saying. Amongst the few fans downloading the odd songs, millions are purchasing the real McCoy online or offline, from the nearest store. These two aren't gonna be broke just yet.

Your stuff is still selling in the hit parade.

There is protection and overprotection. There is Art and the banking world. These two can be interlaced. That's life. When the sheer ignorance of some manage to merge the two into one big cash machine in such an obvious fashion, there is cause for concern!

related links:

The debate continues on the <u>Y2K Forum</u>, highly rated and controversial <u>Napster</u> the <u>MP3</u> sharing software, <u>818</u> music searches, listen and buy your music online, all things <u>MP3.com</u>, Audio Find a gigantic database of music and artist information, <u>Music4-free.com</u> MP3 search engine.

entry date: 10.06.00

162. "Suck"

"Life is a pot of cherries. Life sucks."

Some could bring the two together and suck the cherry.

Suck is the third most searched keyword amongst the five top search engines. And it's not necessarily within a sexual context. There are "suckers" synonymous with idiots, bastards. Aggressive behaviour. Or even a code name in the programming jargon. They are names of websites, home pages. Sucking thumbs, fingers, hands, sweets, food and life. The most unusual the word or the search is, the more likely popular the subject will be in the virtual world. Take your pick.

related links:

Get <u>suckered</u> is an unreal website about <u>sweets</u> and <u>lollipops</u>, Nature is full of <u>suckers</u>.

We've been there before but it's truly a winner, <u>Bialik Sucker Fly Gangsters</u> on the run. A weird shopping site about fishing and hunting.

entry date: 11.06.00

163. "Fortean Times"

Life, again, is full of mysteries. We know that.

What we don't know is how to go about it.

Sensibly by browsing the web or chaotically straight into the realms of Quantum Physics vs. The Simpsons?

It all depends from which angle one is looking at.

I think the latter would provide enough ammunition to discover oneself from a different dimension.

related links:

<u>Fortean Times,</u>

<u>Beam Me Up.</u>

entry date: 12.06.00

164. "The Universe"

The Universe has moved closer and closer in recent years. So much so that we can feel and touch it. It's all there beaming in front of our very eyes.

We have defined our own place from our own design. We

have the choice and freedom of action. Where the burden of choice lies, a throng of opportunities may result. Go, go, go!

related links:

New Scientist

From the maker of the fabulous magazine of the same name. In-depth features.

Spacezone

The exploration archives. Video footage and images of the space exploration.

Hubble Space Telescope

Explore the entire universe through the eyes of the most renowned telescope in the world.

entry date: 13.06.00

165. "Bowie Banc"

"This will positively change your perspective of banking and the internet...forever! You are one click away from zero TIME banking. "

"And everything you do at BowieBanc has David's digital look and feel; a totally Bowie User Interface (BUI). "

Not available to the World outside the US, unless you're an American or have a tax ID. When I phoned to enquire about this banking nonsense, a bright tosser made me repeat my question 4 times. I've admired Mr. Bowie since 1990, up until the stock market accolade.

Fine P.R. recipes to claim back the headlines. That episode made him the richest man in pop music. I thought rock, like punk music, was a rejection of the material world. Actually: Rock music is, punk isn't. Punk makes money by any means necessary.

The elegant interface saturated by his pictures. I've nothing to say about the design of the site but everything about the concept: a pile of shite. Full marks for banking strategy, zilch for self-esteem. It's like being the Queen of England with your head stuck on a paper note.

entry date: 14.06.00

166. "Broken Links"

I do get a lot of mail. Emails and snail mails. I got many complaints about the delay that many users seem to be experiencing in accessing the previous entries of the diary. Especially those from January. A lot of them needed to be reshaped and many links needed to be readjusted.

We had many broken links. Yahoo was a great provider of broken links, straight after Reuters the news agency. I only half blame them. News is news and they need to be replaced. They could provide a notice and a redirection to an archive page.

Some news is still news in the days and the years to come. Some news is being visited over and over again. That's what the web is all about. An infinite virtual library. So infinite that we seem to lose our links. Lose our connections. Tut tut tut. I'm still not impressed.

Continued tomorrow...

entry date: 15.06.00

167. "Broken Links"

Continued from yesterday.

Databases do exist. Or we just don't care. After midnight, this is another day. Another page in the diary.

Well, I do care and went to the far side of Yahoo and Reuters to retrieve the missing links.

I even ended up faxing them. Faxing! In the days of emails.

The result is more than promising and everything is set for our next showcase. We will even have our own search engine to retrieve all the previous entries of the Y2K Diary. I do, we do and I know you do care too. And that's a lot of dos.

And what do many "do" when they are together?

They do rather a lot! They do do, do, do do.

entry date: 16.06.00

168. "Paki Boy"

Lovers, mothers, curry queens and pakis.

Love & loss in the cut and paste generation...

This unique performance by Jiva, with original sound by Seth Ayyaz incorporates movement, mime and theatre to tell a modern fable of our times.

Jiva is presently touring with the Shobana Jeyasingh Dance Company as their first male dancer. JD

Paki Boy is part of Dolly Mixtures at the ICA, London.

19th of June 2000.

Photography by Lisa@Bluesherpa.demon.co.uk

Box Office: (020) 7930 3647

related links:

Find out more from the ICA

entry date: 17.06.00

169. "Buttocks"

"Don't clench your buttocks so much! It's not that aesthetic when yours aren't that firm."

Buttocks are another great web obsession and not in an erotic content, but purely practical and metaphysical.

One understands.

One seems to always nurture a tendency to put on weight in an extremely undesired edge. Buttocks are an illusion that is best kept behind closed doors. There is more to life than buttocks. Isn't there? JD

related links:

Squats and Buttocks.

?

Buttocks and Hip stretch.

On-line fitness with virtual animated instructors, exercise your buttocks, abs, chest etc. I use it every morning!

Liposuction, when you're desperate and can't wait.

entry date: 18.06.00

170. "Derriere"

As the editor in Chief for the respectful content of this Diary, I've allowed Jane to display another picture of a behind,

(in yesterday's entry), as she would have rather put it.

Since many straight male friends of mine complained that on

the 23rd of March we displayed one male bottom and on the 6th of June, a whole team of rugby men exposing their arses (plural of ass), it was just about right to start displaying a girl's buttocks.

This parade of derrieres is not an act intended to tackle cheapness but merely to embrace life from a different angle. Metaphorically speaking. The rear side of the mirror or the moral of this story need not be taken for granted.

Every story tells a story and every story ignites its <u>backbone</u>.

entry date: 19.06.00

171. "Who's Who"

Very little is known about the origins of our source content. For instance: 99% of the content is generated from users throughout emails, submissions and feedback.

60% have an average age group of 18-30+. The remaining age group is unknown.

20% have heard of us through the National and International Press, whilst 70% discovered the site whilst browsing the web. The remainder throughout our successive showcases.

30% are based in London, 20% in the UK, 30% in the US and what's left seems to be scattered around the world. The total always stagnates around 50,000 hits a week.

In January we began at 5000 hits, steadily jumping to 20,000 by March.

Over 100 emails prompted the debate over MP3 music being available for free, the bottom palaver, and the April issues of Internet connection and Free Speech on the web.

The Y2K Showcase moves according to the user interaction.

entry date: 20.06.00

172. "Serious Business"

England won against Germany and I didn't mention it at the time! Apologies. Now that I've finally acknowledged football, I can move on to some serious business.

One such is our next Showcase. Will it be non-virtual or both? The truth is I don't know. Not until next week. We've also decided to mention the details only on the site. Testing. Testing.

The next item will be the grand return of the first six months of the diary entries. All of them are retrievable throughout our home-made search engine. No more going back and back and back only to realise that the next one on the line has been temporarily removed.

Does anyone remember Jane sordid test leading to her even more embarrassing web site and Thumb Sucking in Adults?

Both sites prompted hundreds of emails of dismay and horror. We've nearly had a boycott of our site on our hands. On a global scale that is. I was not amused!

entry date: 21.06.00

173. "Watching"

58 Chinese people died because they tried to enter the Promised Land.

They have paid a fortune to be smuggled into Britain, but Death On Arrival was waiting for them. Only 2 survived. 58 died. It resembles a bad lottery draw.

We live off China and Asia: all the things we buy off cheaply are manufactured there. One always assumed that the Chinese were paid. No slave labour. Otherwise they wouldn't have been tempted by the Western Wonder, would they? We mirror the world to our own image. It seems thus obvious to cross through the other side.

We don't let them. We can't. We'll be swamped otherwise. The virtual world can, but the non-virtual world can't. Time transportation would be the answer. But it's too early. We have to wait. The world is too slow. Far too slow.

Let your views flow... **Y2K Forum**

entry date: 22.06.00

174. "Camomile"

Also, <u>chamomile</u> with an "h" but I prefer the first spelling.

A daily dosage of <u>camomile</u> tea is a must for a fluent and flummoxed blood circulation.

It can help with sleeping. Having said that, I replaced my dosage of morning coffee a year ago with a mug of <u>camomile</u> tea. (2 tea bags per mug)

It can help curing nerves, arthritis, lose weight, stupidity, fertility, timidity, gullibility, vitality, flexibility, *masturbity*, absurdity, nudity and fatality. To name but a few.

The official <u>camomile</u> online presence,

The <u>hilarious</u> and the <u>useless</u>,

Ordering <u>chamomile</u> online,

<u>Contains</u> calcium, vitamins etc., more Facts.

entry date: 23.06.00

175. "Fat Cats"

Fat Cat was a name given to all the big chairmen, ministers and presidents of this world who wouldn't know the difference between one and zero. Take the managers of the collapsing London Underground: one wouldn't be surprised if they were running the damn misery from a different world. They are not there: they take their cut, let the sordid nuisance run by itself and enjoy the sun in the Bahamas. Do they know or Don't they?

The debate is open on the **Forum**.

For instance: Does the chairman of <u>British Gas</u> know that during my last film shoot, Map of the Universe half of my crew and cast fainted because of a gas leak? Do they know that a herd of gas men smelt the gas and went away?

They couldn't smell any gas. Do they know that specialised equipment is needed to detect a gas leak? Only after a major phone call to everyone, the press and the threat of court action, they've finally come back and detected a major gas leak. The same week, a similar gas leak caused the death of 3 people. "You're safe in our hands," says the slogan.

It continues tomorrow.

cntry date: 24.06.00

176. "Fat Cats"

Continued from yesterday.

Knowing how they force their new found clients to open an account with them, even if one doesn't use gas. The excuse given was some outstanding charges because the metre was expensive to install inside the house. A metre that had been installed long before one moved in. But they will still send the bill for it. One certainly wouldn't dare to not pay. They would take anyone to court otherwise. It's amazing, but it's true, it's all true.

The debate is still open on the **Forum**.

There is new legislation coming out soon. Soon cannot be soon enough. The plans are to provide an official website to shame them. The trouble is, one must compile a truly accurate list of misdemeanours. No nonsense and of course, one must be able to prove it.

In the meantime, the only way to bounce back is to log on the keywords in the search engines. Shame > list > outlaw > fatcats > chairman > manager > then the country > place. Alternatively, one could play around with one's leader. Dress him up, tell him off or slap his face off.

Lesson one: Phoney Blair.

entry date: 25.06.00

177. "Tomato"

The anti-tomato website.

For all those who hate tomatoes.

News of the weird and life seen under a third dimensional angle.

If life is a jar of ketchup, then the future is a tomato juice that will render the likes of Julie Burchill, Hilary Clinton and Madonna's best friend sperm donor into diced tomatoes for spaghetti con pomodoro and verdi pesto.

This portal site will transport you to all the different sweetness this fruit can offer.

As the slogan proclaims: "We live to uncover the silence"

entry date: 26.06.00

178. "Watercress"

Watercress is high in protein, calcium and iron. An excellent alternative to meat. Watercress is an English tradition.

Though common on the continent but not so much widespread: it has often been associated with meningitis and left undigested ever since.

" ...high in protein,

calcium and iron. "

I'm a fervent consumer. Ideally chopped or diced and sprinkled over rice, pasta or mash potatoes. Not to be cooked, otherwise all the nutritious components would fade out alarmingly fast.

related links:

Eat nature.

Indonesian Spinach/Watercress Soup

entry date: 27.06.00

179. "Garlic"

" A clove of garlic

a day will keep any

doctor unemployed. "

Garlic has a long history of traditional herbal use as an all-purpose healer, antibiotic, parasite killer and detoxify(-er). A clove of garlic a day will keep any doctor unemployed.

It is an excellent source of chromium, phosphorus, selenium and thiamine. Prevents heart diseases and like chamomile will bring the blood circulation up to date.

It is also an antidote against witches, whoever they might be!

Related Links:

Hudson Valley Garlic Festival - Sept 23rd and 24th 2000.

A Small Garlic Press, a publishing company bringing forward the voiceless. Facts about garlic.

entry date: 28.06.00

180. "Onions"

related links:

The source information.

Top of the Onion, a fan club.

The Onion, satirical weekly newspaper from Wisconsin.

Portrait of an onion girl.

Orange County Onion Harvest Festival.

Onion Head Monster, the famous scary comic, everyone ought to treasure.

entry date: 29.06.00

181. "Potato"

Potatoes come in all shapes and sizes, Jersey, Royal, Imperial, General, Fanatic, World Dominator and Monarchic ones.

The Aztecs and the Incas had a good upbringing on potatoes. Rich in vitamins and minerals, one can grow very fast on them. Well, the South American natives didn't manage to keep their empire, but that's only because the evil Europeans came, conquered and killed everyone.

How alarming it is to witness that my favourite vegetable is the source of so much animosities and *hatrance*.

And I will not mention the Irish potato famine!

Potatoes could become a health problem if eaten in excess in the form of oily chips or French fries (the latter is in fact Belgian).

What ever happened to the Potato Heads?

related links:

World Potato Congress.

Another site documenting the Great Irish Potato Famine.

Potato Head Art Gallery (highly recommended).

entry date: 30.06.00

182. "June Showcase"

Where is this damn Showcase?

Today, we will have our third showcase of the year. At 22:00 GMT. The theme is live underwater. It has been six months since Y2K and another six months to go to Y2K+1. We have introduced new features:

The Diary Search enables the user to retrieve any previous entries in the Diary by date and name. Y2K TV is the web board for all multimedia related activity, operational on the 5th of July. Y2K Club (03.07.00) enables the user to get up to date information on Y2K and anyone can have a free nominal or anonymous email address. My name@Y2K Diary.com.

The Forum is still there, getting as popular as ever and Y2K Chat is scheduled for the 10th of July. The last of the features is Y2K TV Live! After a series of successful and unsuccessful trials it will be operational in August.

July

entry date: 01.07.00

183. "June Showcase"

Here we go. Menu.

1. 22:00 GMT. Presentation of all the new sections.

2. 23:00 GMT. <u>The June Showcase</u>.

An answer to the theme of "<u>Live Underwater</u>".

3. 00:00 GMT. Presentation of the <u>Y2K Diary</u> listings enabling the user to search back previous entries since the 1st of January which will soon have facility to search by keyword, date, etc. It will be the first time that an entire diary will be fully searchable. Some, for instance, have never seen January and February and some can't even remember them.

A myriad of umbrella sites already exists, though they've never been fully integrated in the <u>Y2K showcase</u>. One such is <u>Y2K movies</u>, a presentation of films in a fully interactive form.

The whole integration process will take place on the 1st of September for the next showcase. The showcase will only be available through its new address at **Y2KDiary.com**.

Life is evolving in front of our very eyes!

entry date: 02.07.00

184. "Non-Virtual Retail: Traditional Shop"

On the 5th of February, I severely savaged Marks and Spencer. In fact, since the supremo of French giant Carrefour took the lead, they seem to have improved.

They seem to have cut down on extra packaging. They've introduced food. Well, more food one understands. Now, they have become a food store. For the first time, I could find food that I actually wanted to buy. And indeed, I did.

C&A UK have shut down most of their stores with the loss of 4,800 jobs. At long last! I couldn't see them going on forever with their logo that has never improved since prehistoric times. A logo is the supreme image of a company. If an image stagnates, then it can only die. It's criminal. Not to mention all the jobless.

C&A gone, enter IKEA. Opening new shops and hello to 10,000 new jobs. I know that the entire world will be against me on this one, but I hate IKEA.

Continued tomorrow...

entry date: 03.07.00

185. "Non-Virtual Retail: Traditional Shop (part 2)"

Ikea is renowned for its non-existing customer service relation, neck in neck with the <u>Royal Mail</u> and <u>Telwest</u> (Cable London). Their overpriced seventies/eighties furniture, yet to be placed together with furniture, are yet to be found in shops lost in the dust of the suburbs. In spite of all of this, <u>IKEA</u> is booming. Well, good luck to them.

I have mentioned <u>Cable London</u> earlier. This priceless communication company is running an elaborate scheme: charging all their customers £25 for a phone bill lost in the post. This seems to have reached unprecedented proportions as complaints are now clogging the 'shaming' websites. **Whether or not they send the bill in the first place or whether it has been lost by the customer**. Whether or not it is an elaborate scam, it is certainly a prolific coup. Full marks for sales strategy!

The <u>Royal Mail's</u> huge billboard campaign tells us that: "their customers don't complain, they simply go away". How true that is. The grand motto of their customer relations is: "If you haven't received a letter, it is simply because the sender did not send the letter. We're not in the business of losing letters!" As simple as one, two, three.

Ends tomorrow...

entry date: 04.07.00

186. "Non-Virtual Retail: Traditional Shop"

I wonder what <u>Cable London</u> would say about this. But the Royal Mail, still one of the most fantastic postal systems in the world, does lose letters and sometimes hundreds and thousands of them.

We've recently witnessed an embarrassing episode where we've realised that letters and parcels sent to us never actually arrived at their destination. Even those sent recorded! We discovered all this quite by chance, because we were expecting an important recorded package, sent 3 times.

It did raise the alarm bells. Lord knows how many more vanished in the landfill sites overfilling Britain to capacity. After 2 months the Royal Mail is still 'investigating' and still reassuring us that "if the sender did send the letter in the first place, then the letter would be here." As simple as one, two, three.

The distribution has now resumed and we do get our mail, but the missing mail remains a mystery. ED

entry date: 05.07.00

187. "New Designers.The Future of Design"

Part 1:   6 - 9 July

Part 2: 13 - 16 July

For the 15th consecutive year, the <u>Business Design Centre</u> in London is delighted to be giving 4000 of this year's hottest graduate designers the opportunity to meet you at <u>New Designers</u> this July.

New Designers is the UK's largest graduate design show exhibiting work from 100 UK colleges within 15 design specific pavilions over two dynamic weeks. I remember reviewing their show in the mid-nineties. I've been back every year ever since. It's amazing to realise how many new talents are yet to be discovered.

(Industry Pass £12 for unlimited entry and unique entry £7.

Phone: 0870 735 2100.)

entry date: 06.07.00

188. "Options"

Mark my option.

Select the following option.

The options to choose from are often far too overwhelming.

entry date: 07.07.00

189. "Rhythms of Life"

Saturday 8th July 2000 until 7th May 2001

Monday-Saturday 10.00 - 17.50

Sunday 11.00 - 17.50

Until this day, I've never dared to venture into the Natural History Museum. I thought it was either too far away or that I could easily download my answers from the web. How wrong I was.

"Are you a day person or a night person? How do birds know when to migrate? Why do cows sleep standing up but only dream when lying down? Why do humans get fatter in the autumn? Why might the sound of rock music be like a rainstorm to toads?"

This exhibition's interactive displays reveal nature's true spirit and mysteries. The precise reason for life is being revealed in front of your own two bewildered eyes...Life has never been so unreal!

Adults £7.50 Children FREE (up to 17. Dream on)

over 60s free, concessions £4.50

Hotline: 020 7942 5555

entry date: 08.07.00

190. "Force Field: Phases of the Kinetic"

13th July - 17th September 2000, 10:00-18:00 daily.

Tuesday and Wednesday until 20:00.

<u>Force Field</u> redefines the 'language of movement' in twentieth-century Art. The development of new scientific theories, from Einstein to the <u>Big Bang</u>, has had a profound effect on perceptions of the physical world.

This exhibition explores relative motion, space and time, invisible energies and cosmic dimensions, in the work of over 40 pioneering artists, from Alexander Calder, Laszlo Moholy-Nagy and <u>Marcel Duchamp</u> to Jean Tinguely, Takis and Gordon Matta-Clark. The whole list is <u>kinetic</u> enough.

Booking: (020) 7 928 3144

Entry: £6

Concessions: £4

related links:

<u>About kinetic energy.</u>

entry date: 09.07.00

191. "Chit Chat Week-End"

Chit-chat is according to the scientific community at large, a thorough waste of time. A mere one sentence-briefing could be more fruitful. In retrospect, judging upon my painful days clogged in endless boardroom meetings with media darlings, they might just have a point there.

It was truly a complete waste of time, resources and communication. The right communication does not come that easily, it certainly won't in an environment such as a boardroom.

Nevertheless, I do enjoy my chit-chat with friends on the phone, catching up with the latest gossip.

Online chatting rooms gathered momentum in recent years and this chit chat frenzy enticed me to create my own one for the Y2K. A different chat than **the Forum** and the Y2K TV web board announced for mid-July.

Continued tomorrow...

entry date: 10.07.00

192. "Chit Chat Extended Week-End"

We will have one in the next month, but the Y2K chat rooms will be just right. 3 dimensional. In the broader sense of the term. It will be a multi-purpose game.

I haven't seen many around yet but we will mention them.

One such is iSketch. The Shockwave plug-ins need to be downloaded. The chat enables the user to draw anything and let the "chatted" guess what it is. Different windows for different interactions and different games. Sounds pop up every now and then. iSketch is bringing substance and functionality to chat.

Chat is all we need!

entry date: 11.07.00

193. "Tom"

The word "Tom" comes in all shapes and sizes.

'Tomboy" is a girl who behaves in a rough boyish way.

'Tom" is an ordinary person taken at random.

'Tomfool" is a foolish person.

'Tommy", a British private soldier.

"Tommy-bar", a short bar for use with a box spanner.

"Tommy-gun", a type of submachine-gun.

"Tommy-rot", non-sense.

"Tomtit", a tit.

"Tom-tom", a primitive drum beaten with the hands.

"Tom", a furtive voyeur.

I'm sure the list could go on and on...

entry date: 12.07.00

194. "Spontaneous"

Spontaneous can mean almost anything. I'm spontaneous.

When my research is done, I'm ready to give the diary to the world.

Sometimes, I may be too spontaneous and I have to clean it up a bit afterwards. **Live**, that's what it is.

And if "live" isn't there, then it's stagnant and well beyond reach.

Spontaneous is more often reflected in the spoken language.

Some do "Queen English" (posh).

Some are from Texas and they kill before they can speak.

Some are resolved to slang while others utter a pile of gibberish.

I'm currently working on a gibberish dictionary.

Slang dictionaries are hard to find and yet they do exist!

related links:

Richard Smith's Compendium of Briticisms.

Kerouac's writing advice.

Hear and read Scottish slang.

Cyber jargon.

entry date: 13.07.00

195. "Comics"

I grew up on comics.

Too many comics are bad for you.

The first time I ever read a real book until the end, I was 20! There are thousands of comics available on the market. France and Belgium seem to dominate the market with their diversity. In the U.S. science-fiction comics were incredibly popular up until the early eighties and they remain the kings of animated cartoons.

One such is Valerian and Laureline, space to time agents. Created in the seventies and early eighties, one of the only few science-fiction comics that intelligibly describes the future.

Adults may more likely understand all the references implied in the stories. The original text is in French, but most of the series have been extremely well translated in over eight languages including English.

entry date: 14.07.00

196. "Communication Breakdown"

It's a mental breakdown ... in 5 points.

3. The same problem seems endemic at my Blue Bank online. I wonder if I should start to delete their entire system to demonstrate the leakage in their system.

5. And during all this time on the phone, the proverbial waiting messages are accompanied with the top 10 in what music can make anyone puke beyond redemption during all the hierarchical transfers all the way to the only person who seems vaguely to know anything. One has to find this person, it takes time.

2. Then I spent another two hours of virulent bickering with an internet service provider named after the devil, about a security issue. I'm very far from being the ultimate IT supremo, but I can easily go through their "secure server" and steal or delete their files.

4. It certainly doesn't make one feel very secure.

1. This morning, I spent 2 hours arguing on the phone about

the facts of life with the likes of Cable London.

Continued tomorrow...

entry date: 15.07.00

197. "Communication Breakdown"

Communication Breakdown (Part 2)

It's a mental breakdown...

The points continue from yesterday.

4. Two weeks' worth of mail in some distribution centres gone virtually unreported in the papers, let alone digital TV.

2. And hey presto, this time the reason why we didn't get any mail for two weeks is due to a general strike. The same one they had last month and two months ago. As much as I sympathise with their problems I still need my mail.

1. When I finally got out of the lab where I work, I went to Upper Street in Islington to pick up my mail.

5. The truth is not a long harangue but a serious breakdown in communication. We are in serious danger of...Losing the frame of things.

3. No doubt they wouldn't be able to sort out all the backlog and the mail will end up in the bin. This will become a missing mail.

entry date: 16.07.00

198. "Smoking Kills"

Well, in the land where industry and money speak volumes above everything, this will be overturned.

As much as I'm not a friend of the likes of "KKK fags" Philip Morris, despite their insistence that these alleged days - though they've never confirmed them either - are over and they do not fund anti-gay campaigns anymore. They are convicted for the wrong reasons. Why do people smoke in the first place is everyone's business? I don't. Then again, I do other things. I eat too much and then I have to diet a lot. Some do drugs. I don't. But then again, it's a private matter. We all know the consequences of all these bad habits.

As for smoking, I always knew the dangers ever since I could read the sign on the label: "Causes painful lingering death." That's explicit enough.

Continues tomorrow.

related links:

Old Reuters news. Latest news.

entry date: 17.07.00

199. "Smoking Kills (part 2)"

"U.S. tobacco firms are facing a $145bn bill for damages."

Apparently, they have been sued because "they" knew all along about the devastating consequences of smoking.

Well, like the crappy food we sometimes have to indulge and the air we breathe. What about suing all the Prime Ministers and Presidents of this world for the state of life on the planet? This is their handiwork. In anger, I eat. Some smoke. The same idiots (PMs and Presidents) used to say: "Just say no!" I can't. It's <u>human nature</u>. But if I get my hands on them, they'll be bound for a good punch-up. It won't change the world, but it will certainly make me feel a whole lot better.

I go and visit <u>Her Majesty the Queen</u> when I can't control my anger. The web can be an excellent therapy. If it doesn't do the trick I'll fly to <u>White House</u>. And I'm in <u>Heaven</u>.

related links:

I'm expecting to be next on the <u>Queen's Honors</u> List.

I think I <u>deserve</u> the medal for bravery.

I don't drink, but this requires <u>Tenant Super Lager</u>.

My <u>dad</u> is from <u>Glasgow</u>.

entry date: 18.07.00

200. "The Fruit Family: Citrus"

Freshly squeezed fruit juices are hard to find.

Most of them are ok.

Value / basics / savers juices of the world are exactly the same as their branded counterparts, the difference of course being the label and pictures.

Organic juices taste awfully nice and are higher in vitamins, though it all depends on how one is accustomed to the traditional branded stuff and how one's body reacts.

In fact, cartons are far better than transparent glass or plastic containers, as vitamins will fade away once in direct contact with light. Freshly squeezed or not, kept in fridges or not. Brown glass containers are perfect, but unfortunately most of them have been withdrawn as the consumer thought the colour was far too unappealing to contain decent juice.

A home juice a day from a blender is an excellent alternative.

One can mix organic and non-organic and still stay alive.

related links:

 Citrus family magazine. Growing the fruits.

entry date: 19.07.00

201. "Citrus: Grapefruit Juice"

The grape of all fruits.

Like its brother the lemon, there is also a sexual connotation to it.

related links:

The famous Grapefruit diet.

I'm not endorsing a pill diet but maybe one could investigate.

Grapefruit used in drugs. Grapefruit recipes.

Where does this sexy fruit come from?

Some Grapefruit related facts.

entry date: 20.07.00

202. "Citrus: Lemon"

Lemon, in some weird and deviant way, seems to attract a sexual connotation.

Lemon is higher in Vitamin C than orange.

It's more acidic but with a little fruit sugar (no common crap, please, not even brown) it's a twist too high and high to be cherished in awe!

related links:

Lemon is also a shark.

More about the shark.

What to do with a lemon (scientifically speaking)

entry date: 21.07.00

203. "Comics (part 2)"

"R. Wertz is the writer, artist and sole proprietor of Mad Curry Comics, in addition to eating curry Wertz enjoys the taste of human flesh."

"DEGENERATE ELITE: The DE is a super-secret organisation dedicated to the preservation of the human organism."

I still love comics, though I don't read them as much as I used to. Comics and cartoons are an art within an art. One requires patience and extreme dexterity that I lack and it pains me. I rather like Mad Curry. I'm not too sure what it is all about, but it is certainly intriguing.

According to the information on offer it has been designed by a multimedia company, which has a link to a page with another intriguing message black-out-of-grey, "SORRY!!! This Web Site is temporarily down, ..." The sign has been there for weeks. Could it be that there is a subliminal message behind?

related links:

The Mad Curry site.

entry date: 22.07.00

204. "The Real Slim Shady (part 1)"

"May I have your attention please, may I have your attention please, will the real slim shady please stand up, I repeat will the real slim shady please stand up.... we're gonna have a problem here..."

"I should download her audio on MP3. So, I have been sent here to destroy you and there's a million of us just like me who cuss like me, who just don't give a fuck like me."

related links:

Visit the official site.

Peruse all the Lyrics at your leisure.

The real fan site.

entry date: 23.07.00

205. "The Real Slim Shady (part 2)"

<u>Eminem</u>, the band behind the song has been branded as yet another gangsta rapper from America, with the difference that this rapping on techno-rock-rap music boy is white with bleached hair. His producers are black. The whole combination seems interesting enough.

In 1999, I hailed <u>Fat Boy Slim</u> for being one of the best "things" to come out of that year. There is life after life. Though I find rap music annoying and a whole album could easily make my stomach play some unwanted intestinal sound, The Real Slim Shady will generate slightly different noises.

For a start, it's very video orientated and only works as a result.

Everything you need to know about the message is explained in the video. Therefore, if you like the video, then you'll be more inclined to buy the music. And if you don't you'll still be buying 'into the music' because you[1]re watching the video.

related links:

Visit the <u>official site</u>.

entry date: 24.07.00

206. "Virtual Reality"

Apparently, William Gibson was the man who invented the phrase Virtual Reality in 1981. Or was it cyberspace?

However, this word has existed in French science fiction comics since the 50's. Most probably in the English language as well.

Gibson is considered as the father of cyberspace. I never could understand why myself, nor have I been able to read his books. They lack substance and innovation. What seems to be new to him is already old, gone and buried.

Not many people would share this analysis and Gibson is by and large highly recommended. Still, "Neuromancer" and "Burning Chrome" are mildly enjoyable, even a five-year-old would be able to read them.

Johnny Mnemonic is part of "Burning Chrome." A short enjoyable novel transferred to a gruesome Hollywood state of the crap.

entry date: 25.07.00

207. "QTVR"

As a grand rule, we never use plug-ins within the diary.

We wish to bring a clear and open message as readily and accessible as possible.

However, QTVR (QuickTime Virtual Reality) is a free plug-in that enables every image to be turned to a 3D panoramic landscape.

I will strongly advise downloading it. As we will present a series of images in QTVR in August. We use the software on the image to produce stunning QTVR images and animations.

It's a truly extremely very effective tool!

entry date: 26.07.00

208. "On MTV 2"

MTV has so many digital channels, so they can finally just about cater for everyone's tastes. However, the drawback with MTV2 is that some fantastic artists, such as Coldplay with a brilliant video, shot on a beach, are virtually unknown in music shops.

Like many, they become video hits only on the alternative

MTV. If they don't survive the 2nd and 3rd video, it's unlikely that they will make it in the mainstream charts.

[Picture: Will Bankhead].

There is no shortage of incredible video, AKA artists, musicians, film makers, film directors, editors and all the rest of them.

We're living in an era of creative outburst.

entry date: 27.07.00

209. "On MTV 2"

It's almost impossible to enlist all this talent in traditional media.

That's exactly what the web is for.

I'll certainly mention as much as I can.

Despite many requests, I still can't bring myself to mention Moby.

He's a brilliant mind, musician, video artist, animal defender etc.

I can't listen to him anymore, his songs have been overplayed and the reverse has got bad, bad side effects. I might listen to him during the next revival.

related links:

A bit of online Moby.

entry date: 28.07.00

210. "VA: Short for Virtual Alien"

I've got a website, of course, though it is purely an informative minimalist presentation of my career to date. Nothing ground-breaking there. I'm working on a flash site, but this will not take place until at least September.

As for your interest, I feel the same; I always carry this urge to find out who's who behind everything. Sometimes it is not easy.

For instance, within Y2K Diary.com there are other predominant figures, but they seem to be far more discreet than I am.

I'll leave them! Wait and see. V.A.

related links:

About kinetic energy.

entry date: 29.07.00

211. "It's in Your Head: Into the mind"

26th July - 30th September

Daily 10:00 - 17:50 (Sunday 11:00 - 17:50)

Jerwood Gallery at the Natural History Museum

Booking: 020 7942 5000   Entry: £6.50 Concessions: £4.50

What goes on in my head and what goes on in yours are totally 2 different things. Though, I wouldn't mind going inside your head.

It's in Your Head is an Art exhibition on scientific research into the mind by UK artists aged between 16 and 22.

Art and science come together to look at the source of creativity and invention for artists and scientists alike - the human mind.

It's in Your Head features the best work from ten Arts centres in the UK. Different media has been used: electronic imaging, sculpture, photography and video installations.

Perception, memory, visual interpretation, chemical communication, visual ambiguities and substance abuse are some of the issues addressed.

entry date: 30.07.00

212. "Richard Ashcroft"

We know he was in a band before. The Verve.

This outstanding solo artist, guitar player and performer has at least one stunning video (A Song for the Lovers) to his credit. Solemn, dark, ambient, suspense, silence, beauty, perspective. It reminded me of a scene in Stanley Kubrick's Space Odyssey.

The two pieces of film have one thing in common; they both have been shot with a 35mm Panavision camera.

The song is equally stunning and so is the album.

related links:

His official site.

About kinetic energy.

entry date: 31.07.00

213. "Michel T. Talbot's Bookmarks"

Who the hell is this guy?

I've no idea myself, but his site has got an impressive list of bookmarks and would like to share it with us.

Science, IT and science-fiction are on the menu.

It's really nice to place a whole list of crucial books on the web.

These days it's near impossible to get them from tutors in Universities (Britain, that is).

Everyone is complaining that book lists are either out of date or not available in the country or simply bad.

That says a lot about the level of teaching. I mean what I say.

I've suffered enough and suffered to hear so many fellow students from different colleges moaning about the *crapness* of the system.

Thank heavens we have the web!

Michel T. Talbot's Bookmarks is highly recommended.

Some of the links are missing, but then again with the web it is to be expected unless it is a commercial site.

August

entry date: 01.08.00

214. "Napster.com Gone and Back"

I've said as much before: I'm not impressed.

Why be scared stiff of <u>Napster</u>? Napster is a consumer choice.

Fed-up with over-priced, overrated albums and force-fed hits?

Yes. Napster has the answer. It's the start of a beautiful dream.

On-demand choice, not on-demand force-fed choice. There is a fundamental difference. Don't misunderstand me. I'm not supporting bootleg, but I'm a fervent supporter of choice and quality music.

Napster is not dead, long live MP3!

The debate continues in the **Y2K Forum**.

Continued tomorrow...

related links:

For all the latest <u>Napster</u> news.

entry date: 02.08.00

215. "Napster"

(...continued from yesterday.)

This time MP3 is here to stay. Choosing the track, we really want, not chosen by overpaid record executives who can't differentiate a "Doh" from a "C", or DJ's sponsored by the music label. Still, MP3 sites and music labels will have to give in and work jointly together: tracks will have to be made available for free in order to sell some and short samples will have to be playable for free. The price will have to be accessible and measured according to the huge number of web surfers, that's a hell of a lot of people.

Album charts are killing music as most are pure rubbish!

The debate continues in the **Y2K Forum**.

entry date: 03.08.00

216. "Anti-Nazis Versus Yahoo"

Yahoo got sued by L'Union des étudiants juifs de France/Union of Jewish Students of France (UEJF) and Licra (Ligue contre le racisme et l'anti-sémitisme/League Against Racism and Anti-Semitism) the French organisation against racism about their unwillingness to remove listings for Nazi groups and memorabilia on the Internet.

As much as I have no sympathy for Nazis who would, given the chance, barbecue me for many reasons, the anti-Nazi leagues are often very wrong in their approach and can do even more harm than their enemy. It is best to leave the Nazis to stew in their own juice in a given and known location, where one can oversee them from a distance rather than drive them underground.

The human and animal race like the rest of the vegetal kingdom can only exist with all its varieties.

I won't say "If you can't beat them join them" but don't encourage them and don't run their P.R. for them.

(Continues tomorrow...)

related links:

The debate continues on the **Y2K Forum**.

entry date: 04.08.00

217. "Anti-Nazis Versus Yahoo"

Public relations require extreme tact, diplomacy, willingness and kindness. Some ideas are better than others are.

Some get more publicity than others do and in the aftermath of this sewing business, millions of Nazis turned to the web in search of fellow fascists and memorabilia -or just curious surfers- over clogging the whole system to capacity.

Not so many went to visit anti-racist sites.

Their ratings suffered a big blow as a result.

One could say that Nazis around the world have benefited from a deluge of free publicity. I wish they could understand.

"The medium is the message," Marshall McLuhan.

related links:

The debate continues on the **Y2K Forum**.

entry date: 05.08.00

218. "New York Comedy Network"

When I used to live in New York in the late **eighties**, I went out to comedy clubs all the time.

There are so many of them. My friends would take me to so many that by now; it's ever so hard to remember the name of the places I went to. Thanks to Heaven we have the web to memorise and visualise the past, the present and the future. Even if the entertainment might have somewhat a different feel than a live performance in a nightclub. In New York, a live performance on the web is by and large far more entertaining than a live one on today's digital TV where the multitude of channels seems to have rendered the meaning of the word entertainment into force fed repeats of unwanted, unneeded potentially harmful parasites.

Create your own interactive story online by joining into the story. Chat, dive and discover the New York comedy scene. Now, whenever I need to go back in time, forward or backward in the New York circle of Comedy clubs, I know where to go.

related links:

New York Comedy Network.

entry date: 06.08.00

219. "The Dog's Bollocks"

The Dog's Bollocks so described is our two-monthly newsletter. This is how it has been called by some of the media gurus. If they have loved and enjoyed the showcase, I'm not sure what they have thought about the gobbledygook worth of news we force-feed the media community.

It could be called like the tremendous recent video, song and album by the Red Hot Chili Peppers: "fornication".

Better than one of the heads of the Observer newspaper, when she so un-PRly described the Y2KDiary as: "direct competition"

Oh Dear! I couldn't put it out!

entry date: 07.08.00

220. "What Does KMFDM Stand For?"

Usually, an acronym for a band name is secondary to the name, but in the case of KMFDM, the acronym IS the name.

Originally meant to stand for "Kein Mitleid für das Mehrheit", which translates to "No Pity for the Majority", it has been bandied about and turned inside-out, thought by some to stand for "Kill Mother F***ing Depeche Mode", amongst other possible definitions. (I'm a big fan of them)

"Karl Marx (lots of dictators there) Found Dead, Masturbating" "Kill My Foaming Dog, Madam" "Ketchup My Fries, Don't Miss Kick My Forgotten Doggy Mess"

The writing on the wall never lies.

related links:

 KMFDM

entry date: 08.08.00

221. "Big Brother (part 1)"

1984 wasn't too far-fetched. Everyone who suffered under a dictatorship of some kind could vouch for that.

But the 20th century saw the dawn and shaming of dictators.

The introduction of CCTV cameras now spread to every street

corner, other public places, and toilets, everywhere in fact. Some, would you believe, are linked to the web.

All this in the great name of protection (and security). It's real time TV.

By making the world a safer place one has transformed the planet into a far scarier place.

entry date: 09.08.00

222. "Big Brother (part 2)"

The show is then relayed live on the web and edited for TV, or it could be the other way around. The viewer can vote anyone out and the winner gets a few thousands of pounds.

A cheap way to get the ratings up and it works.

Live action from fresh, hardly paid faces seems to be the ultimate crave of standard TV executives.

Do they pay any royalties to the relatives of Georges Orwell for using the name? I think not! The show has been on air for weeks and we waited that long to talk about it. It shows.

Big brother is also a tremendous song taken from the even more tremendous 1974 post-punk album from David Bowie "Diamond Dogs," a musical inspired by Orwell's book.

entry date: 10.08.00

223. "Big Brother (part 3)"

The Big Brother Directory.

Monitor interaction between nanny / babysitter and child. Covert and hidden video cameras for home, business and office needs.

Provides mentoring services for boys in need of a positive male role model.

Big brother sucks. Message boards for U.S. TV show.

The first unique portal access to all the BB shows in the world.

The big brother system and network monitor.

Source code for Unix and Linux v1.4h.

The Insidious Big Brother Database. Utility for Emacs which is integrated with Emacs and Unix Netscape mail / news readers.

Big Brother UK TV show message board.

The Portal for CCTV cameras linked to the web.

Cyber-Liberties. American Cyber Liberties Union.

"The debate about the role of electronic surveillance in our democracy is as old as the telephone."

George Orwell.

1984.

I'm scaring myself off.

entry date: 11.08.00

224. "Big Brother (part 4)"

It's like my **Est** TV show: I'm locking the contestants for one month in the dark in order to cure them. I interview them every day.

entry date: 12.08.00

225. "Big Brother (part 5)"

I've been told off for saying that Lenin was a dictator. I'm not sorry and I'm unrepentant.

His bust was and still is, I believe, standing inside the loony Town Hall of Islington, North London. Or is it Stalin? The only thing between my flat and Lenin is the bottle bank overfilled to capacity since last year.

Actually, my memory is playing tricks with me: appalling sites tend to imprint my mind too easily. The whole shebang (bottle banks, cans etc.) has been removed altogether. I immediately inquired about this kidnapping. Apparently, they had too many people like me complaining that no one could be bothered to empty the whole nonsense.

With a government who is spending nearly £10 million advertising on TV asking people to recycle when there are virtually no facilities, no collection and never thought of creating a market for it, is it money well spent? Why Big

Brother got it so wrong? Why do we pay taxes? I've been asking the same question all over and over again since I was little but I've obviously never got the right answer so far.

Between Hell and the Deep Blue Sea.

related links:

How to be a good dictator: Stalin forever.

entry date: 13.08.00

226. "Big Brother"

The News of the World in Britain named and shamed convicted paedophiles on their front page. Even those who never committed any crimes were shamed. A whole country has been turned into turmoil, the real offenders driven underground well beyond trace, a witch-hunt-burn-them vigil went on everywhere, new lists came out from nowhere and innocent people were beaten.

During all this huge P.R. palaver, the real questions were never answered. Why do we have thousands of youngsters as young as 10 living rough in the streets of London and all main cities in the world? Why have thousands of youngsters been abused in the care of local authorities for years on end without barely any official apologising, recognizing or even changing the system?

We can never put a face on the abusers. Let alone a name.

We never know where we can find them.

entry date: 14.08.00

227. "Diving Underwater (Part 1)"

After weeks of harangue and gobbledygook we can finally dive underwater again.

entry date: 15.08.00

228. "Diving Underwater (part 2)"

Isn't that nice?

related links:

Huge amount of beautiful <u>underwater</u> / sea photography.

Voyage to the bottom of the <u>seven seas</u>.

A trip to a <u>blue</u> and colourful new dimension.

Main picture taken from the film: <u>Map of the Universe</u>.

entry date: 16.08.00

229. "Diving Underwater (part 3)"

Enter the Life, diving into the blue water of the pool and having a swim.

"I remember. I remember it all well...

In my general state of being, I couldn't be more confused;

I was at times uttering various rigmaroles without even being aware of it. People automatically assumed that I must have sprung from another planet. I couldn't bear trying to go through the whole drama again. Once upon a time, originally, I was born, and, and, and..."

related links:

A guide to under-water photography.

Water search with dogs (?).

Main picture and text taken from the film: Map of the Universe.

entry date: 17.08.00

230. "What else could I do?"

Anyway, the other end of the receivership would have not

been interesting in the story of my life in the first place. So why bother? Why are they purposely disturbing me that way?

Perhaps it was a mistake.

It is a small world indeed.

Of course, one has to be careful not to sound and appear over-refined when first exposed to the world. We never know, we might inflict that lips-sealed feeling or bewildered rigmaroles on the receiver's end and one does not wish that to happen.

Between hell and what, not heaven but the **Deep Blue Sea**, perhaps?" **Pause**.

related links:

The Physics of diving. Highly recommended.

Photo Gallery. Dive and dive again.

Main picture and text taken from the film: Map of the Universe.

entry date: 18.08.00

231. "Diving Underwater (part 5)"

"It has been, in all, a tragedy, but a tragedy worth living for. Heaven is nowhere, where the whereabouts of the unknown is. If only I could, I would dive into it once more. I have no senses left. Only my own derision. This is how I get through things."

"I did not used to enjoy the present day or present moment, and now I cherish them.

I have created an unhealthy torment, this kind of absurd behaviour that no one wants to know or pretend it wouldn't exist."

"A hypocritical judgement and somehow I seem to enjoy it. Perhaps not. Who can tell? I can't. I can only try to get over it. I'm a Philistine, and a true one. This is no devil worship, but a young Britannicus in full compulsion of being."

related links:

A glossary of scuba diving medical terms.

Main picture and text taken from the film:

Map of the Universe.

entry date: 19.08.00

232. "Diving Underwater (Part 6: Final)"

"I've dug my own soul out of myself and don't know exactly what that makes me, but what is sure is that it gave me a rebirth, a feeling of incisiveness, of freshness, as if I were born again. One should always look for the cause of torment and pain if one is trying to remove its symptoms; only then, would one find the solution to all troubles."

"A bit corny, perhaps,

but it's true. It's all true."

Three-dimensional reading always implies a near subliminal message skulking behind the writing.

What we see and read is not necessarily what it seems.

related links:

A dictionary of water words.

Jules Verne twenty thousand leagues under the sea.

Main picture and text taken from the film:

Map of the Universe.

entry date: 20.08.00

233. "Albert Camus. The Existentialist"

The Stranger: A Novel on a Man in Revolt.

An analysis by Linda Drajem.

"The Stranger by Albert Camus was published in 1942 when the author was twenty-nine years old."

"The setting of the novel is Camus' beloved Algiers where he grew up in the poor, working-class, Belcourt section. In many ways the main character, Meursault, is typical of the Algerian youths Camus knew. Like them, and like Camus himself, Meursault was in love with the sun and the sea."

Camus was an existentialist. Aren't we all?

related links:

A documentary on The Existence of Albert Camus.

Everything you need to know about existentialists: an extremely neat, concise and resourceful site.

entry date: 21.08.00

234. "Mirror (part 1)"

The other side of the mirror or the rear side of the story.

" Mirror, mirror on the wall, who's the fattest one of all? "

"If you can relate to the above saying, you are not alone. Thousands of women and an increasing number of men look in the mirror every day and hate what they see."

"I chose to use the phrase 'Mirror, mirror on the wall' because I first heard it used in a fairy tale. Fairy tales are not real, just like the image you see staring back at you in that mirror is not real. When you look in the mirror, you are seeing what your eating disorder wants you to see, you are not seeing the true picture."

"Eating disorders affect millions of people, thousands of which will die from them yearly. There is good news though, eating disorders can be beaten."

"You do not have to be a prisoner to this anymore."

related links:

A complete resource library on <u>Mirror, Mirror</u>: Eating Disorders.

entry date: 22.08.00

235. "Mirror"

The other side of the web is the reflection seen through a monitor.

This language so described has an argument on its own and the user joins into the debate and interacts according to the flow of emotions expressed, challenged and channelled throughout the story.

A website has many mirror sites. A parallel site. We have over 100. Different names, same content but different servers. All the sites reflect unique content. They are all linked to one point. Central point. The mirror image of one single entity.

Thus, we are effectively everywhere at the same time.

related links:

A complete resource library on <u>Anthropology</u>.

Try this one: <u>Y2KShowcase.com</u>, and this one: <u>Y2KTV.com</u>

(now obsolete).

entry date: 23.08.00

236. "Mirror (part 3)"

I still do not understand how mirrors work. I've searched, and looked hard into the mirror...

related links:

A mirror resource library from <u>NASA</u> Grizzle's space gallery.

A <u>Mirror Art Gallery</u>. "Mirrors on the Wall" consists of large water-colours, sometimes combined with oil paint, that represent philosophical or symbolic ideas in the form of stone walls.

<u>Bodyicon Fear</u> and loathing the mirror.

The <u>American woman</u> is pursuing the dream of a perfect body: a scientific answer to why an image of an object is obtained by reflecting it in a mirror so that the signs of one of its coordinates are reversed.

<u>Trick of the cards</u>.

<u>Playing Chess</u> against its mirror image.

entry date: 24.08.00

237. "Mirror (part 4)"

...I dived so deeply into the mirror that I've managed to go through the other side. The mirror was smashed to smithereens and my head bled all over the place. I needed to be transported double quick to the nearest hospital. My head needed 16 stitches. Not my idea of crossing the line to a different dimension.

related links:

The mirror is anti-hallucinogenic: when a therapy patient is actively hallucinating, he is asked to look at his image in the mirror and to focus constantly on his image.

Exercise with your mirror: when we rise in the morning one of the first things we usually do is look into the mirror. What are we looking for? Possibly to see if we are still the same person that we put to bed the night before?

The Mirror mystery: the mirror explained.

The Kinetic explanation: to the mirror image.

Left and right have been switched around. But up and down are not. I am right handed, while that guy in the mirror is left handed. But, he is not standing on his head.

entry date: 25.08.00

238. "Vexillology. The Study of Flags"

The flag has its own language.

The flag shows anyone's true colours.

I haven't made up my mind between the millions on offer.

CRWflags.com is devoted to vexillology. The study of flags.

Here you can read more than 6900 pages about flags and view more than 12,500.

I find it truly fascinating. I'm afraid I still haven't found mine. Mars and Jupiter are missing.

related links:

The study of flags.

entry date: 26.08.00

239. "Naked Bodies"

In the spirit of the summer with sea, sun and sex, we had a look at a torrid period in advertising, in a desperate attempt to use sex to sell otherwise dull and mundane goods and services.

The first in the series is Robbie Williams in a mass marketing campaign. He is offering his naked body.

related links:

The site of Robbie Williams is truly good, neat, innovative and not centred around his face and misleading image. This might help bring Robbie out of the boy-band manufactured label.

entry date: 27.08.00

240. "Naked Bodies (part 2)"

Click ass... and get the bottom line on mortgages.

The above image is not promoting a mortgage company.

Though "Click ass..." is the slogan of Creditweb.com offering mortgages on the web.

The above image is promoting the holiday division of the publishing company EMAP Metro. Bargain Holidays.com.

related links:

Bargain Holidays.com a truly useful site! And CreditWeb.com.

entry date: 28.08.00

241. "Naked Bodies (part 3)"

<u>Acupuncture</u>.

What is it?

I think it's a fashion company. I'm not exactly sure as their web site does not carry the above poster seen on the streets of London.

In fact, the intriguing website does not reveal anything at all.

One can contact a list of worldwide distributors. Take your pick.

Full marks for fashion statements!

related links:

<u>Acupuncture Footwear</u>, licks your fashion.

entry date: 29.08.00

242. "Naked Bodies"

Ideal advice against sunbathing! Direct Line insurance.

entry date: 30.08.00

243. "Naked Bodies"

Robbie Williams is showing his red butt freshly spanked accompanied by a little mate on posters covering London's walls.

Is he either:

a. Trying to prove that he is a straight lad.

In this case by overdoing he may bring across that he is in fact pretending, thus covering.

b. Showing his obsession for naked male bodies and male asses.

c. Showing or pretending his self-arrogance and strong image.

The message is unclear.

entry date: 31.08.00

244. "Naked Bodies (part 6)"

"You need to be naked to enjoy Tango."

Tango is a fizzy drink with an after (or before) taste of orange.

The message is meant to refresh.

September

entry date: 01.09.00

245. "Data Protection"

The aim of the campaign is to empower the individual to use the law to protect their information.

The ad says: "If you're looking at their details, who is the person looking at yours? You have the right to protect your personal information."

Why choose the middle of the summer, when no one is paying any attention whatsoever, to launch such a crucial campaign?

In reality, the citizen (subject if you're in the UK) has few rights. Anyone can obtain anything from anyone. Everyone has got his own black list and uses it accordingly. It's all on the web!

entry date: 02.09.00

246. "Summer Festivals (part 1)"

All through the summer, the world is covered by festivals. With an Onion or Garlic flavour.

I didn't go to Edinburgh this year as their media lectures from last year ruined my whole festival and I dreaded returning this time.

Why do so many boring, out of action farts (media speakers) feel the urge to recite a manufactured future, as their lack of knowledge indicates they know nothing about what they are babbling about.

That's media for ya! The Edinburgh Fringe Festival is still the greatest.

Oasis had bottles of beers thrown at them at the Paleo festival in Nyon for leaving the stage after only 30 minutes. Conflicting news as to the real cause of the problem. Liam, of course, couldn't sing. Basically, Oasis as a whole weren't happy to be there and Liam couldn't be bothered. Not many do these days!

entry date: 03.09.00

247. "Summer Festivals"

The world's biggest Love Parade in Berlin produces tons of live sperm and tons of rubbish, this annoying a lot of Berliners.

But even the most German puritan would rather be remembered for a huge orgy than World Wars 1 and 2.

London's Notting Hill Carnival gets an average of 2 million revellers celebrating the West Caribbean sun.

entry date: 04.09.00

248. "Summer Festivals"

Whilst millions of street parties burgeon around the planet the most embarrassing and irksome of all is undeniably the Islington International Festival (the website says it all).

A bunch of local drunkard hooligans rendering enchanting evenings into dire misery.

The borough that propelled Tony Blair to stardom and invented **Loonyland**, is well trendy because chaos is trendy. On top of the chaos list is the Glastonbury Festival with a highly digressive performance from David Bowie in front of 100,000.

I thought the V2000 festival was impeccable but their site is very strange. There is a near complete list of all European festivals. Check eFestivals list for all the summer events in the UK.

entry date: 05.09.00

249. "Data Protection"

The booming business of personal data means that there is a high demand for databases and there is always someone willing to sell, if the price is right.

It is thus possible for anyone to tarnish anyone's reputation beyond redemption. Being constantly updated with often grotesque information such as: "Living in a dodgy borough, has been broken into 5 times, but always managed to refinish his flat." (Extremely useful information for gangsters and for insurance companies to increase the premium accordingly)

"Registered in a County Court for failing to pay an outrageous phone bill." The case has not been resolved and no convictions yet but it implies that a person is not very prompt with payments.

Oh, dear! Let the Y2K bug strike!

entry date: 06.09.00

250. "Marketing Death"

After being trapped on Monday in the tube for hours and then being evacuated by paramedics ...

... yesterday's excuse, for suspending the Victoria line for hours, was Death.

According to the London Transport, people are committing suicide almost twice a week by throwing themselves under the tracks near Seven Sisters. Why Seven Sisters?

How come nothing has ever been reported in the news?

Death was a common excuse used by the accountant community to justify missing deadlines. "My sister / brother /

father / mother / aunt / uncle died" or combination when they were really late.

It's not pathetic, but unhelpful and extremely damaging to London's reputation.

entry date: 07.09.00

251. "Respect Madonna"

<u>Madonna</u> is still the absolute gay man's best friend and is undoubtedly one of the greatest American business women ever. <u>Who's really behind her?</u>

entry date: 08.09.00

252. "Phone Check"

<u>Everybody</u> needs what everybody wants. But <u>everybody</u> cannot afford what everybody wants. Aye. There's the rub!

The Y2K year has seen a dramatic increase in the cost of phoning. Reports tend to relate to all the major players.

Phone bills are made extremely hard to comprehend with changes then credits then re-change then prices of calls almost doubling the agreed tariff.

In most cases phone operators, after complaints have been sent to the relevant operating body, Oftel, agree to amend the bill.

Some like the troubled Cable London (Telewest) always respond with very patronising and rude arguments to defend their method of random billing. "You've received a bill, you must pay or else."

I would strongly advise anyone to use his/her computer to dial a number. All numbers can be logged including the date and the duration then can be matched accordingly with the relevant tariff. It seems that it is the only way these days to counteract fragrant malpractice.

One would still need to spend a few hours to analyse and digest a phone bill.

entry date: 09.09.00

253. "Pornography"

The unspoken word and most commonly uttered of the Internet, finally out. Should it be banned? You must be bloody joking!

If the world's prudishness equals that of hypocrites, then war and hunger is just a mere flint with human nature.

What people do is their own business. I'd rather leave people to their own orgasm instead of meddling with a subject which is not of my concern and that I wouldn't understand anyway.

According to Yahoo and Alta Vista, about 80% of the people searching the web are looking for it.

I may not be too happy to see a bunch of ridiculous attachments in my emails but I'd rather see a weird picture than a civilian in <u>Bosnia</u> being killed by a gun made in Britain!

Look to the **Y2K Forum** for more discussion.

entry date: 10.09.00

254. "Life on Earth"

<u>Is there life on Earth?</u>

entry date: 11.09.00

255. "Life on Earth"

<u>The Biosphere</u>: Life on Earth.

Understanding the <u>three domains</u> of life.

Is anybody out there?

<u>The New Scientist</u> magazine explores the subject.

Did <u>Earth</u>'s life originate on <u>Mars</u>?

<u>Scientology:</u> a brilliant organisation in desperate need of reforms.

<u>Usenet on organised religions</u>

entry date: 12.09.00

Y2K Diary [12.09.00]

256. Life on Earth (Part 3)

The search for extraterrestrial intelligence.

Is there life anywhere else but Earth?

How life began on Earth is not yet clear.

entry date: 13.09.00

257. " Life on Earth (Part 4)"

Use NASA's site to search for who wrote the book of life?

The microbes were the first inhabitants of planet Earth.

Huge index to Science Fiction Anthologies and Collections.

entry date: 14.09.00

258. "Life on Earth (Part 5)"

Towards an Earth Charter.

A list of reviews and reading about life on The Blue Planet.

History of life, a huge and extremely well-resourced site.

entry date: 15.09.00

259. "Life on Earth (part 6)"

Scientific facts sheet about <u>Mother Earth</u>.

"Roommate Q: I'll ask the questions here because my roommate said he was an expert in this and didn't want to embarrass you. First, what is an obstruction to the 2nd law of <u>thermodynamics</u>?"

<u>Radiation and Life</u>. Radiation is energy travelling through space.

Fast track to the <u>moons of Jupiter</u> - and the key to life on <u>Earth</u> - a prehistoric lake nearly 3 miles beneath the <u>Antarctic</u> ice cap.

entry date: 16.09.00

260. "Time. What Time Is It?"

3) Central European time (in WW2) is forward one hour from GMT.

I'm hardly a good <u>time keeper</u>.

I don't wear a watch, never have been and never will. I just can't. Anyway, I have a psychological notion of time.

I can't measure up to the minute, the second but I round it up every two hours.

I measure the tempo of my music when I practise an

instrument. That's about the only time I dare to interfere. No one invades my time without my approval (Theoretically).

entry date: 17.09.00

261. "Time. Lost in the Dust of Time"

Swatch divides the day into 1000 beats.

One beat = 1 minute, 26.4 seconds. Noon = 500 beats.

This revolutionary new unit of time means the following:

No Time Zones, No Geographical Borders.

I still think time must be challenged and can be easily regained.

It's only a matter of knowing when to stop and break with the treadmill of life.

entry date: 18.09.00

262. "Time. Time Takes a Cigarette..."

New Earth has invented a new common language of time where the day is divided into 360°. 360 earthbeats every day, 15 earthbeats in an hour and 1 earthbeat every four minutes.

The world is time obsessed, too scared to die of boredom.

Some say that boredom is a modern invention.

I can't quite abide by this statement.

Boredom belongs to those scared of the next best thing to come.

Time takes a cigarette and transmutes to ashes then to dust.

With time everything fades away. That's the magic of it.

entry date: 19.09.00

263. "Hackers"

Apparently, this site is known to support and fund illegal activities with criminals.

Antionline.com, I thought it was a well-resourced site about the problem. But the real question is who the real hacker is

and who's the real enemy. Who creates a virus? Who is misusing the system, accidentally or intentionally? Who, by sheer stupidity and cost-cutting, has so many security flaws and contemplates denial until it goes too far?

In issue 196 (14.07.00) of the diary, I was so angry I actually threatened to "enter their system and do something horrible."

A week later, they've publicly half acknowledged the problem by merely muttering that it was a recent problem.

I saw the problem on day one when my Blue Bank went online. Although they have annoyed me severely throughout the years by their proverbial stupidity I never hacked into their "open and easy access" system.

entry date: 20.09.00

264. "Hackers"

A lot of <u>American hackers</u> (more ingenious than I am) first highlighted their findings and weakness of some systems to the relevant authorities and have been met with a barrage of laughter.

Frustration and anger seem to be the drive of a lot of these "criminals". I think it's high time to start taking the problem seriously and treating these "fault detectors" as some

kind of genius and use them accordingly. But one thing is paramount: when leaks are detected to the relevant bodies, they should finger them as criminals if they start laughing as they are themselves the first cause of the problem.

entry date: 21.09.00

265. "Hackers"

"<u>The Hacker's Defense Foundation </u>is a Not-for-Profit foundation dedicated and committed to the advancement of the hacking community, through education, of the social, political, and legal implications of the uses of technology, and seeks to enlighten the public and law enforcement about the hacking community, through education, that hackers are not the lawless goons that law enforcement, the news media, and Hollywood would try to portray them as."

"The Hacker's Defense (UK: Defence) Foundation does not condone, support, or defend criminal acts."

entry date: 22.09.00

266. "Hackers"

The Good Hacker's Guide:

The Hacker's Defense Foundation.

The History of Hackers.

Hackers Emergency Response Unit.

The hacker test.

Hire an expert hacker to protect your system.

Hackers Hall of Fame.

Try and understand. No one wants one's treasure to be looted. No one wants chaos. But: what no one wants is some idiots working in a major corporation or government body to continue to poison everyone by their sheer stupidity, lack of communication and disability with IT. As long as they are allowed to continue, there will be more and more virus infected systems.

entry date: 23.09.00

267. "Hackers (part 5)"

The Good Hacker's Guide

^^^^^^^^^^^^^^^^^^^^^^ by Bruce Sterling.

HAO, "World Industries is a small organisation of computer-guru from all walks of life. Some of us are network administrators or Internet service providers, while others are Linux, Unix, Mac, and yes, even Windows fanatics. Despite our differences, we have come together to work toward educating society. We openly support the Open Source movement and encourage our members to embrace the movement's ideals."

"Here are some basic truths about the system and the people who run it. I am including this section first to dispel the rumours floating around. In particular, I'd like to direct this section to the wonderful individuals affiliated with the Federal Bureau of Investigation (FBI) who have a misguided interest in us. Worse, they have been told many of these points repeatedly by friends AND foes of Attrition, yet they will not accept the answers."

"No, we are NOT a hacker gang. We do NOT hate mongers. We are NOT an FBI front, nor anything else industry charlatans like to call us. We ARE hedonists, sick little monkeys, and the people our mothers warned us about."

entry date: 24.09.00

268. "Communication Hacked (part 1)"

I lacked for many years the great Art of communication.

Life is a business and every business correspond to another business from an equal and opposite force.

I've discovered and experienced bad, appalling, greatly exacerbated and no communication at all. Distorted and false communication came into it as well. Deafness is an added parasite. It takes a great deal of investigating and a thorough understanding of society to be able to analyse the causality of problems, honest or dishonest thriving from breakdowns in communication.

Acknowledging that history wouldn't have been made, if it weren't for all the dramas and mistakes the human race can generate. There is a point of decency where a proper debate should question some of the prime structures of our modern society.

We must accept any guilt. We have the right.

(Continues tomorrow...)

entry date: 25.09.00

269. "Communication Hacked"

In the digital age the entire communication semaphore is more profuse and unscathed, omnipresent and constantly challenged on the Internet.

The beauty of recollection and transposition into a data or into text is the ability that the user or reader might feel compelled to decipher this rudimentary and elementary piece of communication: the language.

This language, so described, has an argument on its own and the user joins into the debate and interacts according to the flow of emotions expressed, challenged and channelled throughout the story.

The user / (reader) becomes a player.

Erasing the distance between the signifier and the signified, between the thought seeking to express and the expression.

entry date: 26.09.00

270. "Autumn Leaves"

A rounded naked woman seen from the back is the latest desperate attempt from the struggling food store chain Marks and Spencer to regain some kind of moral ground.

I've seen the posters on the billboard: trashed, painted over and ripped to pieces. **Oh Dear!**

Straight women do not enjoy seeing other naked women, especially rounded parading their derriere.

Gay men do not find it very enticing.

We are talking here about their long-term customers of course.

Straight men rarely ever shop in women's shops and lesbians would feel deeply offended by the Ad.

Would all these offended consumers agree to endorse MS <u>tag</u>?

As the slogan says: Hallelujah!

That's one advertising agency out of the way.

Would Mark's get a refund?

entry date: 27.09.00

271. "Autumn Leaves"

E) They don't think of it as being <u>autumn</u>.

It is very rare to see a <u>smiling leaf</u>.

But when you do, it's <u>beautiful</u>.

entry date: 28.09.00

272. "Autumn Leaves"

"This food-making process takes place in the leaf in numerous cells containing chlorophyll, which gives the leaf its green colour. This extraordinary chemical absorbs, from sunlight, the energy that is used in transforming carbon dioxide and water to carbohydrates, such as sugars and starch."

entry date: 29.09.00

273. "Autumn Leaves"

It sold many papers and raised all news ratings to an all-time high but the acting was pretty poor. The chap who played Tony Blair was quite impressive, though. The news on TV was extremely funny too. Panic in supermarkets. No more deliveries. Introducing rationing. I never ate so much during a week.

A week of holiday and revealing for many. X-Mas was early this year. Strikers, car users and the rest of them up in arms. No more tax on oil consumption! Queues and queues of cars waiting and polluting the air, and angrily waiting for a drop of gasoline.

A good thing happened. A feel-good film for many.

"Oil strike" may win an Oscar for the amount of ticket sales.

Memories flow within autumn leaves then all get blown away.

entry date: 30.09.00

274. "Autumn Leaves"

I wish advertising were less dull in the early part of the 21st century.

Repeating the same ad over and over again is killing viewing attendance and driving potential consumers away to other forms of media. Even web ads tend to merge within the site with a constant change of content.

The late nineties saw the emergence of the use of interactivity in a TV commercial for "Esprit". The *tele spectator* was invited to record the commercial and then to rewind its content to discover its secret fast-forwarded meaning.

Then, once the video has been rewound, the content lets one eye a catalogue of their recent collection. I seem to recall that they also did a film version.

It did include the same footage. It wasn't possible for the audience to physically rewind the film, but when with the magic of the cinema brought it to life, the fast-forwarded film version provided an excellent aesthetic interaction that led the audience to believe that it was the content of a catalogue without the need to immediately rewind the picture.

October

entry date: 01.10.00

275. "Autumn Leaves"

"Everyone of us should wear a leaf to cover one's genital region."

Useful leaves:

The Digital Media World show incorporates the Leaf festival: animation workshops and seminars on special effects in Motion Pictures. 14th - 16th November 2000 at Olympia, London, UK.

A beautiful photograph.

Gorgeous pictures of leaves: the problem in composting autumn leaves in the US.

Autumn leaves, wallpaper and screensavers.

entry date: 02.10.00

276. "Autumn Leaves (part 7: Epilogue)"

Recycling the planet in autumn.

An irrational and conspicuous video

> > > > >

[It may take minute or two.]

[848 KB]

Spinning the debris. It's a beautiful time and a very sad one at the same time. Almost irrational and conspicuous. This equinox will last for a while as things have slowed down.

A lot of wankers (masturbators) tempered our space recently. The cleaning is not taking place in spring but right now. Sorting the world out. Keeping only the bare-necessities. Getting rid of all the dastardly cretins of this world. We're nearly there. Goodbye Autumn Leaves...

entry date: 03.10.00

277. "Debris"

Life can be beautiful.

Some debris:

An MP3 music magazine called Digital Debris.

Analysing the space debris: non-profit, membership-based organisation aiming to stop adverse environmental impact of light pollution and space debris.

entry date: 04.10.00

278. "Debris"

Most fashionable debris of the language:

<u>Debris</u>: A group (plural) of morons.

<u>Debris</u>: The last days of the Olympics.

<u>Debris</u>: A group (plural) of arrogant swindlers.

<u>Debris</u>: (quote) Why does it feel so good?

<u>Debris</u>: (actions like) Wondering and pondering.

<u>Debris</u>: (sentences like) One needs a lot of money to live.

Hit List:

- <u>NASA Watch</u>. Scrutinising the sky for space debris. <u>Nasa is still under construction</u>.

- <u>Debris Road</u> - Ocean Color Scene un-official website.

- <u>Cosmic Debris</u>, Vancouver is a really useful magazine for musicians and the music scene.

entry date: 05.10.00

279. "Debris"

Débrisé [de-breaked]. Y2K most famous faux-pas:

Débrisé: When a telecom's company runs up debts of over a billion pounds and still can't run analogue services, let alone digital services.

And when the company thinks it's clever to be sold off to another one and still can't get it right under a new name. Then the need is felt to get another buyer and so on and so forth. What started the problem in the first place?

Débrisé: A major corporation trying to get bigger and bigger under the same name. It is easier to kill or break through a major one than a few companies working together.

entry date: 06.10.00

280. "Debris"

Débrisé [de-breaked]. Y2K most famous faux-pas:

Débrisé: Arrogance and pretension offered by heads of Customer Relations from major corporations. The biggest trend in recent months. No one will be fingered.

Débrisé: Kissing the devil. When in business, feeling the urge to sleep with one's client.

Marine plastic debris. What is the problem?

HIT LIST:

All programming, Html, Perl and various tools. All kinds of debris. A resource centre.

entry date: 07.10.00

281. "Debris"

I understand Israel is often misunderstood.

I receive my fair share of hate mail: "Anyone who refuses to turn Israel into another Iran is the devil and deserves to be crucified". What does it mean?

In another email: "I'm desperately waiting for the tenderness of the likes of Danna International to take over and open Israel to a true multicultural society". That's better already.

Then again Israel is already a true multicultural society.

entry date: 08.10.00

282. "Debris"

Débrisé [de-breaked]. Y2K most famous faux-pas: Débrisé: The Inland Revenue (in the UK) for fining by £100, everyone who has their self-assessment tax form lost in the post. Also, the Inland Revenue (UK IRS) for sending the form after the assessment date and still fining for late return. Débrisé: The Royal Mail for losing a record-breaking amount of mail, even those recorded.

Débrisé: Fox-hunters for justifying their sport by claiming that, like rapists do, the victim enjoys it.

HIT LIST:

An otherwise ordinary human echoing his voice on the alarming problems of space debris. Human Debris, magazine for all into planet Quake.

Crash Debris.com, the history of UFOs in contact with Earth.

entry date: 09.10.00

283. "Debris (part 7)"

Débrisé [de-breaked]. Y2K most famous faux-pas:

Débrisé: Tony Blair for patronising the electorate into plundering nearly one million pounds worth of tax for an ad campaign aiming at convincing everyone not to give money to beggars.

Get rid of them! Thanks, Tony!

The Final Débrisé: Place all the pieces of the puzzle together and discover the game. Our new October showcase in 3D.

- 23:00 GMT Monday 10.10.2K.

By highlighting the mishaps of this world one can only hope that the swinish Débrisé in question will move on and cease being debris all its life.

HIT LIST:

The insurance industry: echoing his voice on the alarming problems of space debris.

Meteoroid and Debris Database: from NASA.

entry date: 10.10.00

284. "w-e-i-v-e-R (!sdrawkcaB)"

After a week of debris, I'm lingering on my days of emotional bereavement over all the nonsense of this world by listening to the new Radiohead (B) album. "Kid A" is a t-r-e-m-e-n-d-o-u-s piece. A slight departure from their previous albums with an anti-Tony Blair twist. A big number one in perspective.

A friend of mine introduced me to JJ72 (C) recently and I thought, well yet another breath of fresh air. Not heavy, but mind filling like Coldplay (C). I've been told not to plug in Bowie anymore, but I have to say that his new double album (D) of all the live performances at the BBC is t-r-u-l-y disgruntling.

I went to see the House of Mirth (A) and I l-o-v-e-d it. An

Arty-costume period drama with X-files Gillian Anderson, directed by Terence Davies. And yes, I've seen Billy Elliot (B), the life of a young lad trying to become a ballet dancer. And yes, I l-i-k-e-d it. And it's not a laughing matter.

Rankings: A-arty, B-brainy, C-cool, D-demented.

entry date: 11.10.00

285. "Spectacular Bodies"

The Art and Science of the Human Body Form.

19 October 2000 -14 January 2001

At the Hayward Gallery, South Bank, London.

Photography, sculpture, video and installations.

entry date: 12.10.00

286. "In Search of Halloween (part 1)"

In my youth as a Goth I witnessed many a fake blood sacrifice and many a defiance of the cross, symbols of the occult. No one cast any spell on me, though I'm not too sure about that. There are two kinds of black magic: The Goth one and the African witchcraft.

Apparently, there is a Goth revival:

Sisters of Mercy, Placebo, Bauhaus, The Mission, and the less Goth but still dealing in skull and skeleton: Motörhead, Virgin Prunes, Black Sabbath, The Damned, Psychic TV.

Of course, the cult films by excellence are:

The Hunger. Dir. by Tony Scott starring Bowie, Deneuve and Sarandon. Halloween 1 and 2, The Exorcist and the trilogy: The Omen 1 and 2, The Final Conflict.

I think these guys have been eating too many magic mushrooms. Enter at your own risk. Astral projection, Black magic, Blood sacrifice, Occult book, Spells, Conjuring spirits.

entry date: 13.10.00

287. "In Search of"

So many books have been written, and yet some are saying that they are in fact tremendous Quakers and devoted human beings, some are saying that they are a bunch of loony fascists believing in an Arian master race. Some managed to survive to this day.

Some useful sites:

A brief history, discover their tremendous castles.

Catharism and the Albigensian Crusade.

A long list of books on the subject.

A tremendous list of different cults, including the cathares.

Bogomil's Gnostic Corner Bogomils were Krstjani, Christians, Patarens and Cathares living in Bosnia and Montenegro.

entry date: 14.10.00

288. "In Search of Halloween (part 3)"

According to tradition, Arthur, when a boy of fifteen, was crowned King of Britain, in AD 516. Soon after his ascension to the throne he founded the Order of the Knights of the Round Table at Windsor. I'm not a fervent defender of opera, but my favourite one is undoubtedly King Arthur by British Baroque composer Henry Purcell.

Some useful sites:

Sir Thomas Malory's Book of King Arthur and of his

Noble Knights of the Round Table, Volume 1.

A Clip Art Gallery? More new tales to tell.

The Legend of Camelot, the magic sword, Merlin and the Holy Grail.

The Literary History of the Round Table.

The Order of the Templars and the Quest for the Holy Grail.

Quest of the Round Table, an adventure card game.

Rick Wakeman composed the Myths And Legends Of King Arthur And The Knights Of The Round Table. (1975)

The screenplay to the Monty Python film: The Holy Grail.

entry date: 15.10.00

289. "In Search of"

"In Voodooland, my Voodoo master makes me tremble, my Voodoo master takes me out of bounds, my Voodoo master can tamper with my soul, my Voodoo master can infuse germs into my system, my Voodoo master knows it all, my Voodoo master can heal my depre-va-tion, my Voodoo master can trigger my sexual appetite in Voodooland."

Some of my most revealing lyrics from Voodooland, 1989.

Some useful sites:

Salem Witchcraft Trials 1692.

A Clip Art Folk Magic in Britain, (1200-2000).

Complete 1692 Salem Witchcraft Papers and Narratives

of the Witchcraft Cases, 1648-1706.

The screenplay to The Vodun religion, history and background.

Witchcraft magazine.

The Center of the Pagan Web.

Cast a spell and play the game.

Sexual Voodoo Shopping Center.

Voodoo's introduction to JavaScript.

entry date: 16.10.00

290. "In Search of Halloween (part 5)"

When I was 16 (in the late Eighties) I had a dark album out called **Old Nick**. In the U.S., it instantly attracted a Goth tag and fans used 'that name'.

It became a bankable name, so my label of the time released the next album and three singles using 'that name' as a band name. I agreed for a while as long as the name would not appear in the UK where people would derive a different meaning. In all, I thought it was a stupid name and I was more, for a while, a camp devil than an all mighty devil legally abusing and swindling the roots of society, like, well, too many conmen at the moment.

Some useful sites:

I'm a heretic, philistine and all the rest of it but this Mormon site is really funny.

Lucifer.com, for your distinguished pleasure.

Devil Worship available on video.

History of the devil.

Devil Worship in the Middle Ages.

The Centre of Law Enforcement in the U.S.

666 the number of the beast.

Pagan festival from hell.

entry date: 17.10.00

291. "In Search of Halloween (part 6)"

Deconstructing the first word HAL.

The super computer invented in the sixties for the film:

2001: A Space Odyssey by Stanley Kubrick.

This became the basis of all human computer interactions.

Some useful sites:

They have reactivated HAL.

A dialogue with HAL.

The legacy of HAL.

Simulator: HAL.

Another dialogue with HAL.

Screenplay to the film: <u>2001: A Space Odyssey</u>.

Scientific American <u>HAL</u> legacy.

Explore the tremendous spacecraft using **VRML** language.

(Requires plug-in)

entry date: 18.10.00

292. "In Search of"

Deconstructing the second word **LOW**.

<u>Low</u> end.

<u>Low</u> fat diet.

<u>Low</u> cost.

The site is from a U.S. band called <u>LOW</u>. Not a hyper trendy site but clear, concise and well documented which is extremely rare.

The <u>LOW</u> Temperature Laboratory, based in Helsinki, Finland.

<u>LOW</u> Probability of Racoons - Peter Howard's site of poems and poetry resources.

The legacy of <u>LOW</u> culture.com. Why web-safe colours suck.

<u>LOW</u> approach.com. The place for aviation databases.

The <u>LOW</u> Vision Information Center is a non-profit organisation that helps people with low vision maintain their independence.

Fyodor Dostoevsky High Spirit, <u>LOW</u> Spirit. A life.

<u>LOW</u> life. On-line magazine for the intellectually challenged.

Explore the tremendous <u>LOW</u> by <u>David Bowie</u> and co-produced by <u>Brian ENO</u> in 1977. The album that allegedly changed the face of music forever.

entry date: 19.10.00

293. "In Search of"

Deconstructing the third and final word, **WEEN**.

[Archaic]

Be of the Opinion;

Think; Suppose.

<u>Ween-y</u> meaning tiny.

The <u>WEEN</u> Official site for this rock band.

<u>WEEN</u> Women's Enterprises Electronic Network from the University of North London.

The <u>WEEN</u> brothers. Are the lyrics respectable?

The Weird Wide World of <u>WEEN</u> E-zine.

Official website of the Hit Comic Book Barry <u>WEEN</u>.

Have A Safe and Happy Mall-o-<u>WEEN</u>!

Hell-o-<u>WEEN</u>. Beware of October the 31st.

<u>WEEN</u>. Open Source Software.

A (New?) Development Methodology.

entry date: 20.10.00

294. "Reductio Ad Absurdum (part 1)"

They say that the world would be a far better place without religion, and the politics that comes along with it.

The trouble is: the world wouldn't function without religion.

Continues tomorrow.

entry date: 21.10.00

295. "Reductio Ad Absurdum"

HIT LIST:

<u>Reductio ad absurdum</u>. Getting the picture.

<u>Reductio ad absurdum</u>. Getting into the spirit of it.

<u>Reductio ad absurdum</u>. Getting into the physics of it.

entry date: 22.10.00

296. "Reductio Ad Absurdum"

The same nonsense can be said about bureaucracy.

I can't believe that the Y2K year has reached a record level of bureaucratic nightmares.

Forms to fill in, attachments, paper and paper and a lot more paper. Remember exactly what you did last summer and the summer of 1990? Who did you shag in 1992? How much did you weigh in 1995? How much will you earn in the year 3000?

And the true flag of political correctness is:

Are you:

a) white (and proud),

b) black (and unhappy),

c) don't know, (this may be used against you)

d) transgender

e) hermaphrodite, f) yellow, g) brown, h) pink, i) legless.

I'm actually e), but I always refuse to answer. I truly think that the process is first degree racism.

Ends tomorrow.

entry date: 23.10.00

297. "Reductio Ad Absurdum"

The sheer debility of this hippy-loony-lefty think tank. Which I once belonged to at some stage, minus the hippy, plus the punk.

Would force whites to come out proud and pure, blacks to be fingered at, gays and lesbians to be <u>outed</u> and disabled to be looked at. Some are resolved to lie, pretend and abide by this ludicrous system. I thought all modern ideologies were based upon freedom of choice. Obviously, I was wrong.

I fully comprehend the need to put facts and figures together. But it seems that there is ignorance on the amount of information requested and an awful number of trees getting slaughtered in the process.

entry date: 24.10.00

298. "Farting"

Political correctness, bureaucracy and Middle East conflict, as well as other targets. Well, things had to be said and I said them.

I haven't seen many courageous people daring to voice that there is a level of decency where absurdities from either side of the equation must stop.

Of course, when conflicts are so deep, marriage is out of the question. Like heroin addicts, one needs a replacement to bite into. War makers and terrorists alike along with their fellow bureaucrats, all need to be recycled into useful means for the process to work.

Standing in the way of this is called farting.

There are many kinds of farting.

entry date: 25.10.00

299. "Something Beautiful"

In the nineties, Gold and Fresh became a stepping stone in advertising motto.

Since one of the best bands to come out of the doldrums of the variety market, -Coldplay, that is- with lyrics such as "Something beautiful", the bandwagon queued up to use the word beautiful.

In music and in most TV, magazines and slogans. The word came in all shapes and sizes. Though its usage existed before, it wasn't as prolific as in this first Y2K year. All the better for it.

We could do with more beautiful things in this world.

Related links:

Pictures of beautiful girls in a tasty but revealing compound.

BRL. <u>The Beautiful Report Language</u>. The whole manual.

<u>BeautifulBoy.com</u>. Gay youth online.

<u>Beautiful People</u>. The movie.

<u>The Beautiful Thing</u>. The movie.

<u>Life is beautiful</u>. The film.

<u>The Beautiful</u>. An alternative band.

entry date: 26.10.00

300. "Hate, the Ugliest Word in the World"

I hate the <u>NHS</u>. I don't see where NHS (UK: National Public Health service) contributions are going.

Obviously not in the health sector. This extra tax is equal to that of private health insurance. Like in the U.S., it covers everything and hospitals do not need hands-out, and there isn't a five-year waiting list for a benign operation. One needs a doctor, a GP. One must use one nearer to one's residence. Depending upon where one is living the doctor is either:

a) In his first year of study.

b) Over 100 years-old, completely senile, ignorant and dangerous.

c) As it happened to me: for failing to use my GP enough, my custom has been replaced and the waiting list closed.

I've tried another one and the same story. The trick is to wait for an emergency and then run to the casualty of the nearest University College Hospital and in the evening or the middle of the night otherwise the waiting time is: 10 hours. Those who can afford are rushing to get their private insurance but are still forced to pay for the NHS. From the most admired health care system in the world, it is now the most hated. I hate those responsible for this chaos and even more for using that word.

entry date: 27.10.00

301. "Pyrrhic Confusion"

When people die a herd of coroners and pathologists too easily conclude that a murder took place, when the person in fact died of a heart attack. Bureaucracy, that's all I can say! How easy it is to end a dossier by putting the finger at **a nobody** when this nobody is getting thrown into jail, thus reducing the crime statistic and improving the confidence amongst the general public. No problem in overcrowding jails.

Now, they are half run electronically, with rotten food being dumped by robots, drugs supplied to top dog barons to keep the denizens in line.

Now, jails are like the good old days of chuckles and straw, mouldy water and rancid bread. If the decor and the props may have changed slightly, the principles remain. The beatings and sexual abuses are omnipresent. For anyone who did or didn't do a thing [in the legal sense] a sojourn to the luxury complex of a terrestrial cage or one of the newly converted boats [soon to be spaceships] will scar the protagonist for life. Although there are degrees of scars and the level of endurance being one great exploit in itself and the level of absorption is another exploit that can never [ever] be eroded.

entry date: 28.10.00

302. "Forming the Future"

I need to know! We do get a lot of mail.

We are currently reaching approximately 180,000 users a week.

It's staggering.

We are ready to announce when/which new section will come first.

The mail we get is great. We know what you want from us.

But now, we need to know in a very limited amount of space, how you feel about us, about the **Y2K Diary**.

- NEWS -

Y2K Club: 01.11.00.

The EDGE Image Bank: 15.11.00,

Y2K Diary search engine: 31.11.00,

Y2K KiOSK: 10.12.00,

Y2K Dimensions (3Dimensional Chat): Jan 2001,

We do have a **FORUM**, but many of you find it too long to register before using it. Some used it a lot during the summer, but for legal reasons we had to delete half of the messages. We are not happy about that, but the law called upon us. Still your messages have been heard.

It's pop-up time again! Please fill in where appropriate.

entry date: 29.10.00

303. "The Young Cripple's Opera"

We are all aware of organised crimes.

It's more disturbing when the problem hits closer to home.

There is a new type of distressing slavery. It all started when a friend and I went to talk to a young boy age 14-15. This boy had no arms or legs. He was begging. He was bruised around his neck with fresh cuts near the extremity of his arm, near his elbow.

We suspected that despite his strong reluctance to talk, he was of English origin. He was scared stiff. After 5 minutes two men came forward threatening us and interrogating us about our interference. We explained that we were trying to help. I can swear that they were ready to take a knife or gun from their jacket. I gave them £20 and they let us go.

Last week, I saw another young legless and armless. I was gutted to witness this. From a distance, I've managed to observe the scene: as soon as a police patrol moves forward, someone is there to pick up this poor soul and take cover. Few minutes later, as soon as the coast was clear he was back in 'business'.

Homelessness and down and outs are one grave problem. International traffic in human lives is another. Continues tomorrow.

entry date: 30.10.00

304. "The Young Cripple's Opera"

On a good spot, they can fetch up to a minimum of £150 a day.

7 days a week, between say 100 young lads, it soon adds up.

They probably get £5 worth of food a week and a few beatings.

It is a relatively new problem.

I have contacted the police, who informed me that they are aware of the problem. They can't act unless they can speak to a victim.

In this day and age, we do not leave children like that in the streets. We can help them to help themselves to some dignity and self-respect. They could possibly have artificial limbs, etc.

Some have been mutilated on purpose. It's not a new evil. It happened in many third world countries. Whatever caused their misfortunes, some are being smuggled into the West (Europe, U.S.) to slave for International crooks. These gangs are powerful. They have 'friends' everywhere. They are lawyers. This problem is not endemic to refugees. Some are from the West. Some have obviously been traded in when they were in the care of local authorities. Some are undoubtedly on the list of missing children.

It's a new but growing problem and a very fast growing one too. **Ends tomorrow**.

entry date: 31.10.00

305. "The Young Cripple's Opera"

Charities are very reluctant to even acknowledge the problem. They've enough on their plate without adding international gangs. It is, as I have experienced, very dangerous ground.

There is not much an individual can do.

Giving money to a homeless person is a personal choice.

To them (the legless and armless) it is useless, though, they might get less beating if they do get some money. I often buy a sandwich every now and then for a local down and out. In this case they would hardly be able to eat it.

The police told me that the best way to act is to call 999. They will then send very swiftly some trained officers to deal with the problem. Crisis in London told me that if they are seeking help, they will receive help. The trouble is, they couldn't do that.

I felt really gutted to be so powerless. I'm also very concerned that, even though this problem is new it is still unreported in traditional media.

Is ignorance bliss? Is it better not to know? Could this person be your missing child? How would you know?

entry date: 01.11.00

306. "Compile and Compare"

Like in France, cinema tickets can be bought for next to nothing. Where are the 3D animated films, digital screens, open-air shows, silent movies, shadows on the wall, *son et lumiere* performances?

Blur made my day with a compilation album celebrating nearly 10 years of radio-friendly music.

On the review package, I'm always flabbergasted to witness the volume of books published on the market, it is also true for games. Some like PlayStation 2 make one feel bored beyond redemption, and it is very annoying when one can't find that last minute game. Ancient games are on the increase. Apparently, a Tarot is more than a soothsayer's game, it's a sensual healer.

November

entry date: 01.11.00

306. "Compile and Compare"

As the 44th <u>London Film Festival</u> kicks off, I'm already desperate for the <u>New York Film Festival</u> in March and the <u>Sundance</u> next year.

Strange, but many people don't even know there was a festival last year in London, let alone this year. Is it the format which is not suitable for a London audience? The content? It's fine by me but if someone calls it the London Film Festival you'd think of a major celebration involving more than just the loony and Arty scene, but everyone. Above all: not just located in the West End!

Like in France, cinema tickets can be bought for next to nothing. Where are the 3D animated films, digital screens, open-air shows, silent movies, shadows on the wall, *son et lumiere* performances?

<u>Blur</u> made my day with a compilation album celebrating nearly 10 years of radio-friendly music.

On the review package, I'm always flabbergasted to witness the volume of books published on the market, it is also true for games. Some like <u>PlayStation 2</u> make one feeling bored beyond redemption, and it is very annoying when one can't find that last minute game. Ancient games are on the increase. Apparently, a Tarot is more than a soothsayer's game, it's a sensual healer.

entry date: 02.11.00

307. "Smashed to Smithereens"

If the <u>Smashing Pumpkins</u> wasn't a <u>Halloween</u> joke and <u>Beck</u> wasn't a beer, then the <u>debris showcase</u> so described many a moon before wasn't an April fool's day and is pleased to be back for consumption.

The pieces of the puzzle were smashed to smithereens and required a dexterous sleuth to put it right.

If the dull life of <u>Smash Hits</u> makes one shiver with anticipation, then the future so described resembles a giant pile of <u>pumpkin cubes</u>.

entry date: 03.11.00

308. "Smashed to Smithereens"

Pumpkin Soup (serves 4)

Ingredients: 1 vegetable cube, 1 medium-size pumpkin (also available tinned or frozen), 1 tablespoon curry powder, 250ml of cream / skim milk / soya milk / soya cream, 2 large potatoes, sea salt and pepper to your taste.

Directions: Peel the pumpkin and chop into small chunks, place in a pan of boiling water with salt and the veggie cube and simmer. After half an hour add the potatoes, peeled and cubed. After another half an hour, the pumpkin and potatoes should break into pieces. Now add the cream (or equivalent) and curry powder. Stir the content into a creamy mixture, adding salt and pepper to taste. Add more cream if needed and leave at a low heat.

Your pumpkin soup is finally ready. **Or not?**

Pumpkin Tart

While making the soup, add an extra portion to the mixture to make a tart. Sprinkle with cinnamon and ground nutmeg (approx. half a teaspoon each). You may need to add some more cream, but at this stage I would highly recommend something skimmed (6 tea spoons) and sprinkle with cane sugar (or fruit sugar) and stir into a sweet mixture.

Put this on a pastry base on a greased baking tray.

Bake on a medium heat for 30 minutes. **Enjoy!**

entry date: 04.11.00

309. "Smashed to Smithereens"

The card game of poker has enjoyed a phenomenal revival in the first of these Y2K years.

You may wish to reverse to diary number 11 to comprehend this subliminal <u>binary</u> logistic.

_ · _ · _   (START)

_ · _ · / · _ / _ · / _ · _ _ / _ _ _ / · · _ /

· · · · / · _ / _ · / _ · · / · _ · · / · / · · / _

· _ · _ ·   (END)

c / a / n / y / o / u / h / a / n / d / l / e / i / t / ?

related links:

<u>Very basic rules</u>.

<u>Poker FAQ</u>.

<u>Articles and tournament dates</u>.

<u>Awful casino style website</u>.

entry date: 05.11.00

310. "F A T"

You are what you eat, remember? One must assume and learn to deal with it. Of course, it's not easy. One has to deal with one's own environment and this environment might be the biggest pile of <u>tossers</u> one can find. The fatter one gets, the more likely one will be bullied and the bigger one will get. Is it better to smoke in excess or to suck one's thumb? Cells grow faster and need more fat in contact with fat. Fat was only created as not to be afraid of one's own surroundings. **Self-defence**.

Some tampered with one's metabolism; some are guilty of the worst atrocities. Parents have a lot to answer for. Is there any wonder why a young kid is big? When one is growing it's much easier to modify the excessive growth of the cells. Of course, parents will have to change and stop dumping their own problems on their children.

Supermarkets and food manufacturers alike have a great deal to answer for. One cannot deny one's own biscuit or favourite chocolate. But they all sell in excess, in multipacks with extra added sugar. (And in times of problems it is very easy to eat the whole pack). 98% FAT FREE is the biggest commercial joke.

Fat replacement leads to cancer and tastes like dog's food.

entry date: 06.11.00

311. "F A T (part 2)"

Slim Fast works but one will regain all the lost fat from the diet. <u>Weight Watchers</u> is a money-making gang promising you the world at an excessive price. It doesn't work.

It will take up to three years to lose weight, WHATEVER THE AMOUNT OF FAT.

In this order:

a) the realisation. b) the acceptance. c) the commitment. d) the progressive exercise routine. e) the nutrition studies/what's what. f) the change in surrounding/scenery. g) the change of lifestyle/TV consumption. h) new hobbies/work. i) maintaining the selected steady exercises (not excess). j) learning to eat less (even if some of the food is fattening). k) maintaining this for three years and beyond. Once this is observed, a routine will take place and the procedure will become a part of life.

One can return to this system whenever weaknesses will be sensed. Lipo-suction is not as terrible as it once was. It's expensive and it would make more sense to send money to a third world charity. One needs to consider lipo with prudence. One must check with a GP for the right one. Lipo will never eradicate the 3 years plan routine. This must be done in conjunction. No more than 2 liposuctions at the very most. More and your general health will suffer and you may encounter many complications.

entry date: 07.11.00

312. "F A T (part 3)"

Exercising can range from running, going to the gym (I hate gym, it can be addictive & dangerous) walking frequently and giving the bus a miss, fooling around with friends or as part of a team in football, martial arts, diving, cycling (in the country), dancing or rambling.

Swimming is the tricky one. Excellent for the heart, it is not a great help for slimming, though even once a week it's a general well-being (max 3 times a week or you will quickly feel bored). Learn to swim on the back, move your chest up front as if you were rowing and fold your knees sideways. This is one sure way to replace cycling and the gym. Swimming 20 lengths is the norm. (Start at ten.)

The lifestyle is connected to an excessive amount of TV trash. The London soap EastEnders is now socially accepted for being a major cause of excessive growth in fat.

Look at the long-standing characters: from thin and happy faces of nearly twenty years ago, they are now all miserable and overweight. 75% of viewers are slouching whilst watching and eating fatty food.

Food is a drug and food are an addiction. But, there is life at the end of the tunnel.

entry date: 08.11.00

313. "Your Good Deed for the Day (part 1)"

Feed the starving.

The hungersite.com is a special website. It shows a world map.

Every three point six seconds, one of the countries flashes black. Each time it is signifying a death due to hunger. The countries keep flashing. The thought is sobering.

Today's deal is how to help feed others. It won't cost you anything. There's a button on the *hunger site* which you click to donate free food. You may click it only once per day. But it's not you who pay, it's the site's sponsors, who as you will see are prominently displayed after the donations made. The more sponsors the more is donated.

Often, it's right to be suspicious of sites like this. Which is why I've spoken to the United Nations World Food Program, the UN agency responsible for preventing malnutrition. It distributes all the food donated and confirms each click does provide food. The *hungersite* has also joined up with two sister sites.

Submitted by: Sokari, London

Continued tomorrow...

entry date: 09.11.00

314. "Your Good Deed for the Day (Part 2)"

Feed the starving.

The rainforest site.com was founded in May 2000.

Each click you make here buys back 4.8 square feet of tropical land per sponsor saving it from deforestation. Though it tends to be less well received than the *hungersite*.

The kids' aids site.com is the newest site in the stable. It was launched towards the end of September 2000. I must admit to being staggered by the statistics when I saw it. Every day 1800 children in the world contract AIDS. It's another powerful image. Each click provides 5 seconds of care for a child per sponsor.

Using these sites can really save lives. The hunger site has an average 5 sponsors a day. Each sponsor pays half a US cent. So, a click is worth 2 and a half cents or one and a half pence. If there are 250,000 clicks world-wide per day, which is good but not exceptional, that means in total the sponsors are paying £3750 daily or £1.4 million pounds a year. Enough to buy just over 6000 tons of food. Saving roughly a quarter of a million people from starvation in that time.

Submitted by: Sokari, London

entry date: 10.11.00

315. "I'm Afraid of the Americans"

Hilary Clinton won her New York seat.

Getting sick and tired of hearing about this election nightmare?

Only 50% of 200 million registered voters...Voted! Who cares?

Who would vote? How can you get younger people to vote?

By lying to them? By ordering a few thousand death penalties?

By offering a gun and a crucifix to every Young American?

If Monica Lewinski would have run for the presidency maybe the other 50% would have voted?

God might be an American.

In the land where money is king and rules the world, the only Governor is oneself. A gun, a damn good lawyer and a few bucks.

By the way, I didn't vote.

I'm part of the young clued-in Americans.

Love ya! JD

entry date: 11.11.00

316. "Playing the Game"

This is a Game Board.

The rest of the story need not be shewn [archaic] in action and indeed would hardly need telling if my imagination was not so cribbed by the sheer lack of objectivity and lazy care for my demented surrounding on the ready to wear slap-dash cocky bitches and pansies in which decadence keeps its toll of natural disasters.

It is thus possible for me to interact in a more cohesive fashion, especially if one user might feel somewhat compelled to forward the diary or move 6 months back. But this is my personal thought and this is merely based on my own assumption that life or the year passing us by is easily moveable, adjustable and reshape-able, therefore flexible enough to be played with again and again.

If ranting on the Bitterness of Being wasn't a state of mind already invented, then this "Great Swindle of Being" transmutes into the biggest cock-up or the flamingly introverted E ever conceived in the history of K.

So there!

entry date: 12.11.00

317. "Design (Part 1)"

How many steps does it take for the spider to dress its linen?

Written and designed by the spider.

entry date: 13.11.00

318. "Design (part 2)"

" ɆᵒNý-Þh¤¶ÁØÇYx+i@üXøÀØ¿Stwq%²=€Vᵒ=`ÀŒè¹"

Written and designed by the spider.

entry date: 14.11.00

319. "Billy Gates, My Love (Part 1)"

I know you're right. Piracy is a crime. But wait, crime isn't necessarily a bad thing. Crime exposes crimes. Crimes trigger debate and debates keep our society alive.

For years I would copy software, I was to a small degree a 'pirate'. A modern Robin Hood. I can't anymore as I'm a registered designer, artist, businessman, however one would define me.

I've mentioned Robin Hood because as much as I love and

admire you, Billy, I have to say that you're a legal crime baron. And that's what I was really rebelling against.

Hence the fact that I was broke and only copied college software, already bought for the students anyway.

All your software had already been bought tenfold before, and was by no means new, you've only slightly modified it. You can't keep on charging for old rope.

You should only charge for the relevant updates, and if your software isn't easily updatable, it should be!

Continued tomorrow...

entry date: 15.11.00

320. "Billy Gates, My Love (Part 2)"

Well, that's only part of the problem, Billy my Dear! I still love you and admire you very much. In many ways I wish I would be more like you. You are very talented. You have changed the face of the world and kept millions of people employed.

What I really deplore is the weird way in which you have designed your software. It is full of micro viruses. One has to be very vigilant. We are all very lucky that the world's networks are not about to become one giant virus thanks to you. Besides, as a programmer and writer, I've chosen to use more logical software. More logical than yours, that is. By trying to be too clever for its own good, Word seems to be losing words and Excel is infamously overfilling one's hard drive with micro-viruses.

I know you're mega successful and that's why I admire you. Though, this stems not from your programming or design skills but your extreme business sense. Of course, you are a Master of P.R. and without extreme P.R., no one can succeed. P.R. is there to convince us about what should be a worthy cause. It helps to keep our minds at bay. It helps not to think about what we are consuming.

More tomorrow...

entry date: 16.11.00

321. "Billy Gates, My Love (Part 3)"

I know how much you may hate Microsoft users thinking about the usefulness, the why and precise why of your program.

And I don't mean to "think different" either. That would be very Islington think-tank and bad English as well. Though. Who really cares about that these days!?

My Darling Billy, why don't you concentrate your research into funding new and I mean brand new software that you can legitimate, resell and you won't have to force-feed us with your old infected words?

Yours frantically,

ED.

P.S. Please continue to contribute generously to Amnesty, Greenpeace, Children in Need and Crisis. It will help you to justify your earnings. **Ends here**.

entry date: 17.11.00

322. "Psycho-Path"

My obsession with food faded a few weeks ago. Though I still laugh at organic food, I dismiss GM food entirely.

I had to stop drinking already squeezed fruit juices. Got too many sore throats. I've resolved myself to take the time to squeeze (with a machine, that is) my juices. [I rinse my fruits first, unlike all of these juice producers. Not to mention cleaning the squeezer every now and then]

Sore throats? Never again!

And I don't blame it on Global Warming either. All the blooming floods have been predicted so long ago that I'm amazed how little and how late there are. Malaria is on the increase in New York, would you believe? In the very country whose potential future leader refuses to recognize the problem, let alone doing something about it!

I'm reading the paperback novel American Psycho by Bret Easton Ellis. Even better than the film.

Continued tomorrow...

entry date: 18.11.00

323. "Psycho-Path"

I've received 54 emails from users complaining about yesterday's diary.

They want to know what I'm talking about.

The world's efforts on global warming have been hampered by American psycho-logical uncertainties about who's winning the election.

If they can't even know that themselves, the state of the world will soon become a giant dire psycho-drama. Like Jane, I'm still afraid of the Americans. I'm enjoying the new live album from Oasis.

More tomorrow...

Tomorrow's diary entry is not suitable for anyone under 18. The world is being reviewed in all its splendour.

entry date: 19.11.00

324. "Psycho-Path"

I might turn myself into another Mr. Bush. Mad, bad and dangerous to know. I'll be feared and respected.

I'll live on psycho-bananas Island. [One can live on bananas]

I'll be a psycho-killer.

All my ministers will be called bananas. When I have to squash them, they will become a dessert-surprise. Almost like a pudding.

My urine will be banana juice, a thicker version will be my sperm and my shit will be white because a banana is white. My farts will smell like bananas.

When I have finally eaten all the bananas on the island, I'll soon suffocate under stacks of banana skins. My last epitaph to the world will be: "Good bye bananas!"

By this stage, the rest of the world would have collapsed, submerged by water and starved by lack of bananas.

If the moral of the story has already lost its ulterior motive, let alone its sense, there is little but bad taste left on this planet.

entry date: 20.11.00

325. "Design"

In part 1 of the science of Design, we explored and asked in how many steps the spider is building her linen? The answer is 6.

entry date: 21.11.00

326. "Tea with the Media (Part 1)"

Monday is normally my media day, and yesterday was no exception. <u>Media Monday</u> implies browsing around <u>London's Soho</u> for the latest gossip in the media world.

I'm still waiting to get an answer on a project from <u>Saatchi</u>

whose recent ascension in the <u>New Media world</u> is staggering.

Is traditional media finally waking up to the future?

I had 3 lunches, which is average on media day, 1pm at <u>Mezzo</u> on Wardour Street with a friend from <u>Fox</u>, then another at 3pm at <u>Valerie</u> with my friend from <u>Sony</u>, then tea at a friend's flat from <u>DJ magazine</u> on <u>Old Compton Street</u>. I had three major disagreements with the three of them over three pots of <u>Earl Grey</u>.

They all had coffee and sparkling water, of course.

(Numerous Masciatti, Latte and Espresso respectively.)

The disagreement came from my lack of tact and diplomacy.

I'm too bitchy and keep on slugging everyone off in the diary.

I strongly refuted all accusations.

[Though, it's true that my <u>Foxy friend</u> was wearing a <u>Paul Smith</u> tie and a <u>H&M</u> suit which is very cheap indeed.]

Continued tomorrow...

entry date: 22.11.00

327. "Tea with the Media (Part 2)"

Whatever happened to blue hair and <u>Alexander Mc Queen</u>'s ensemble? What ever happened to <u>bass and drum</u>?

Has the media lost its originality or have they all moved to <u>London's Hoxton</u>, dyed their hair black and taken to wearing second-hand garments from a bygone era?

No answers from my <u>Sony friend</u>. Too busy sipping his latte. I've tried to argue against his accusations, that I have no skills at all in presentation. He argued that my PR (politically recycled) and marketing package is always unreadable, too vague, abstract or too arty. Well, I nearly got a <u>Sony PlayStation</u> contract. "Yes," remarked my friend, "but you blew it at the last minute by emailing your phone bill when we asked you:"

"How much is how much?"

Well, (again) it was the wrong attachment. It happens. 'She' should have seen that we are reliable, judging by the size of the phone bill! Anyway, full marks to <u>Sony's PlayStation 2</u> PR! "Don't rush to buy PlayStation 2, as due to an unprecedented demand, you may find it missing in the shop!"

Continued tomorrow…

entry date: 23.11.00

328. "Tea with the Media (Part 3)"

It is truly amazing how ads and announcements actually mean something different and everyone will eventually realise that, but we don't want to read the truth anymore.

"Don't buy" means "buy", it just makes us feel better.

TV companies and the music industry as a whole are slowly waking up to the web. For years they saw it as an ad on teletext-style medium before realising the competition it represents to them. BMG (soon to be part of Sony) made a deal with Napster and we know now that MP3 format will be the music of the future and is buyable online. TV companies have started to invest some serious money in Web-TV and Web-radio based formats.

I have been so angered to witness the number of firms, government bodies and councils telling me to check their web sites for further information when in fact their sites have not been updated since last year. I had to phone back to ask for their full postal address because it was missing, as well as a myriad of other items. Most sites visited carry the eloquent: "**Under Construction** " **sign** and I told them this. [This left them a bit gobsmacked.]

entry date: 24.11.00

329. "Tea with the Media (part 4)"

Things do change but at the pace of a snail gliding over the grass. But the culprit is not, as I discovered, the site's designer or the companies that contract the work in the first place.

The culprit is the cohort of 'P.R. Darlings' still at loggerheads with the web, failing to realise and accept its importance and dominance in the media world. After all, companies can easily crash on the stock market simply because of negative writing on a few websites triggering an avalanche of negative publicity in both the virtual and non-virtual world.

In the first quarter of Y2K, 70% of the web was used to find pornographic material [search engines logging]. During this last quarter the figures went down to 60-40%.

I can't believe how extremely well-designed porn sites are. Not purely in the design sense, but within its specific subject the volume of originality, the navigation and impressive e-commerce facilities. It pays! The more content and update generated, the more balanced the web will become. If all of those who complain about porn on the web will stop writing so much nonsense about it, but will start finding new subjects, content and navigation the balance may well narrow. **Ends tomorrow...**

entry date: 25.11.00

330. "Tea with the Media (part 5)"

P.R. does not only require an impressive elocution and an insatiable desire to sell or to blame you, the consumer, if something goes wrong but an extremely acute brain, an extensive knowledge of the world and social awareness, diplomacy and politeness. Some of these qualities are often missing.

P.R. must be enhanced to the point of being able to find and meet solutions. Since P.R. rules the world, dictates politicians and creates the news, it's high time that the qualities I have hitherto mentioned were embraced in order to help our endangered world. Of course, this will never happen as P.R. is there to convince us about what's what and to win the day for the next client willing to play the game and not for the goodness of this world. Still some brain and true continuity wouldn't go amiss.

That reminds me of our broken links. Some ghost websites floating around, some being replaced by another without warning. I decline all responsibility in our web references. They were there on the day but some vanished without trace and without a sign. Some have asked us to transfer their content to our server which is fine. We do have a summary of each website and we will start linking all broken links to one page. Gone? Moved away? Broken? <u>Tell us!</u>

entry date: 26.11.00

331. "Tosspots (part 1)"

Dear Diary,

There's a first, I never called you that way before.

There is a starting point for everything, I suppose.

I'm not having a very happy week. First, I'm desperately waiting on some tosspots to give me an answer on some contracts. Incidentally, they got caught in two months of bureaucracy. On Monday, if they don't get back to me, I'll sue for time-wasting. Time is money, you see. Some obviously don't have to work for a living otherwise they wouldn't waste so much time. Tossers!

The publisher (a big one) for the book of this diary is scared stiff of the web like most of the publishing industry. Old tossers! They asked me to stop publishing the diary on the web. Tosspots! We are a web diary! And a book is a book. Different medium, different entertainment. Tossers!

To add to the bitterness of these unhappy pills, I was invited to an opening of an art exhibition in London, about some crackpot watercolour society or something (no web presence as yet), by the River Thames. The invitation stipulates that mulled wine and mince pies will be served.

Continued tomorrow... (If the tossers will let me!)

entry date: 27.11.00

332. "Tosspots (part 2)"

Dear Diary,

On arrival, a sad <u>tosser</u> urged me to buy a lottery ticket (£5) for their secret funds; I then discovered that the wine and pies weren't free. **Talk about promotion**.

But then, this is not New York or Paris but pretentious London. <u>Tossers</u>!

In the midst of this jumble sale of High Art, I tried to get a glimpse of one of these famous watercolours but more <u>tosspots</u> were overfilling the place to capacity. It was the last straw! I left after five minutes under the pissing rain watching a group of beggars lying down by the river.

Maybe I should get a canvas, urinate on it and sign it, call it "Piss on Canvas" and auction it at <u>Christie</u>'s, then give the money to a homeless charity.

This is **<u>High Art</u>**, the latest contemporary revolutionary culture.

entry date: 28.11.00

333. "Ding Dong"

Dear Diary,

Bush is in. I'm out. Ding Dong!

What will be our last showcase party of the year?

Too late to think of something out of the blue. It has all been seen and done a million times before. Too short notice for everyone, too busy with Xmas and all the nonsense. I thought about singing some carols in Soho, London (maybe SoHo, NY as well, in a sort of mini-tour) with a bunch of friends.

Wearing a kilt (being a Scot, and no, Scots do not wear underwear underneath their kilts). On top of my traditional carols I would of course throw in some of my back and new music catalogue. A cappella. I'll dye my hair red and wear an old Westwood red and white coat with the mark on the back saying "too fast to live, too young to die", or something along those lines.

It goes without saying that all money collected will be given to charity. Minus the expenses, the trip to New York. **Ding Dong!**

entry date: 29.11.00

334. "Hapax Legomenon (part 1)"

(I have mentioned this once before.)

Dear Diary,

It's me again. Don't worry too much about the title. It's Greek. It sounds cool and will be seen many times in the near future.

I have mentioned a lot of things in the past, things take time to develop. In my experience, everything does turn up and everything always pop's up like a Jack-in-a-Box when you're least expecting it.

3D and 4D reviews, freebies, goodies, download, QTVR, VRML stuff may never see the light of day in any future format of the diary. We can't have plug-ins in the diary itself. The extended diary lets you see extended content of the diary in a clearer and more concise format. I've slugged off, demolished and plagiarised many people or companies this year. Do I still feel the same? In the run-up to Xmas we will explore this and try to kiss and make up. Billy Gates will formally answer back to my accusations.

entry date: 30.11.00

335. "Hapax Legomenon (part 2)"

(I have mentioned this once before.)

Dear Diary,

The human will be wiped out by a giant meteorite and an earthquake, drowned by flood, suffocated by <u>Zyklon B</u> Air quality, swamped by bureaucracy, demented by stupidity, rotten by the lottery, crashed in a train derailment.

Most of the above items can be stopped. Every one of them in fact. Those in charge won't understand. Too happy to collect taxes and loot the lot as they go along. It has never changed. Perhaps we should collapse. The year Y2K has revealed that most of us lost faith in change.

Only 48% of registered voters around the world actually vote. Out of it, 16% (believe) to be voted for money, freedom of choice and freedom to exploit (right), 16% (believe) to be voted for social justice, fairer society and bureaucracy (left).

Both tendencies sparkle by their blindness of life.

To be continued tomorrow...

December

entry date: 01.12.00

336. "Hapax Legomenon"

Dear Diary,

Both political parties have no sense of what is right or wrong and have a record of miscarriages of justice, legalised swindles and corrupted nepotism.

16% is composed of extremists, undecided and green *utopists*. The question raised throughout the year was: "How can we get people to vote?"

The answer is: "When the above facts mentioned will be addressed."

But this will never happen. "Live and let live!" This is another answer.

entry date: 02.12.00

337. "Hapax Legomenon"

337. On Thursday evening:

Dear Diary,

Do I have to review the <u>Miss World 2000 Contest</u>?

A parade of brainless bimbos showing their boobs to promote their country! Hosted by dirty old man himself:

Jerry Springer.

Miss Uruguay nearly won and would have had my vote when her final statement was about all the ignorance in the world being the cause of all problems. Miss India won and would have had my vote but she blew it at the last minute when her last statement was: the greatest person in the world is Mother Teresa. Her dad was in the audience, and a friend of mine commented that he was probably carrying a bomb inside his turban.

Later, I was invited to what used to be the trendiest evening of the year: Glitter Ball 2000 at London's Scala. A very boring evening. (I should have gone to the one in Covent Garden). Is this kind of Aids related charity showcase still work? Or is it just merely some eighties nostalgia? Awareness and a solution to the African epidemic are needed. Petty Cash from glamorous evenings is hardly the answer!

Anyway: welcome to the **Eighties revival!**

entry date: 03.12.00

338. Hapax Legomenon (I have mentioned this once before) (part 4)

Dear Diary,

I need to sleep. I'm getting desperate.

I'm on my own doing the work of six.

Everyone is either in New York, L.A. or Paris working and sharing their talent for private use rather than making it public in the Diary. Not to mention that we are moving in the newest and trendiest media Hotspot:

London Canary Wharf.

Where it feels like New York. Forget Hoxton, forget Charlotte Street and forget Soho. New World here we come! We are supposed to celebrate our last showcase of the year coming soon, very soon, when soon is sooner than soon and soon has suddenly lost its ulterior motive. Things are happening; things are always happening. One must keep at it. Overcome all kinds of stabbing in the back. (By unscrupulous devils, communication companies and all the rest of it). Everything converges back to communication. Damn! All the problems encountered during the first Y2K year are about communication and lack of it. Hence the lack of sleep factor. Sleep and longevity, sleep and communication. That rings the bell...

entry date: 04.12.00

339. "Hapax Legomenon"

 (I have mentioned this once before) (part 5)

Dear Diary,

I know I've been bad during the year.

I know I have blacklisted many and have been equally blacklisted. I still despise politicians. I can't change that. I'm not sure they can.

entry date: 05.12.00

340. "Hapax Legomenon"

 (I have mentioned this once before) (part 6)

Dear Diary,

The amount of emails received is unbelievable. I have touched a few nerves. The interaction is in full swing.

entry date: 06.12.00

341. "Hapax Legomenon (part 7)"

(I have mentioned this once before)

Dear Y2K, [to be placed in the right order]

4) Is this diary actually telling anything?

5) Do we need to know that he's an idiot, we pay too many [and too much] taxes and half of it goes astray or she slept with him or him?

3) I know telephone companies have one main problem: communication. That's why they used to be big, now they are small and deep down in the red.

1) Are you trying to settle a few scores through the diary? Or is it Apathy News?

2) There are so many problems these days because of communication. Once we know that, then we either communicate with the right person, even if it does mean running all the way through [in hierarchical order] to the top.

Otherwise forget it! Take the money and run.

A concerned user. Tomorrow: return to normal.

entry date: 07.12.00

342. "The Queen of One's Body"

The once Queen of one's body, Anita Roddick (now dead in 2012 and sold the business to Nestle or L'Oreal (shares))! The founder of The Body Shop has left the oatmeal, hemp and chamomile essence empire to the King of French Yoghurt: Danone.

She was -is- the Queen of conscious driven businesswomen introducing recycling and reusable containers, encouraging Fair Trade with the Third World and an ingenious taste in advertising. Preferring to promote Amnesty International in her shop windows and campaign on human right issues, rather than spending millions on TV ads. Her ground devotion was against animal testing.

Everyone else copied her product and ethics, though more in theory and P.R. rather than in practice. When she came out with: "New fragrance for every Tom, Dick and Harry" with naked men on the poster, she was accused of promoting homosexuality. "Dear Bastard, so nice of you to test on innocent animals in the name of beauty."

Her life story is out now at Amazon or your local bookshop.

entry date: 08.12.00

343. Alea, Jacta Est.

Madonna is undoubtedly the Queen of POP and the web. Her Netcast from London's Brixton Academy may have lasted only half an hour but it attracted 9 million people on the net and is expected to reach 20 million visitors by December 12, when Billy Gates' MSN will close the site. Her latest album, Music is still one of the best of the year in a commercial pop danceable and innovative genre, one understands.

She works hard for the money. She's also well surrounded. There is a whole industry at stake. Don't we all work hard? Aren't we all successful? It all comes at a good time. Aren't we all rich? Well, in my humble experience richness comes in when good communication nurtures good communication. Things take time and even longer in London of all places. Things need to be planned in advance, well in advance. Verified and counter-verified. This is the nature of success. **Alea**, **iacta**, **est**.

entry date: 09.12.00

344. Alea, iacta, est.

Dear Diary,

Julius Caesar first uttered the above title. His ubiquitous presence on the web will guarantee him immortality. He and his fellow partner Cleopatra had a baby. The androgynous oriental beauty and the hard man of Rome. Rumours have been replaced by historical facts about the non-existence of their sexual life.

Who cares? Not me of all people. Julius Caesar must be remembered as a Great general who conquered half of Europe. **PAUSE**. What am I saying?

He might have killed and slaughtered half of Europe. Forget about remembering. Forget about his sexuality. Concentrate on his writing. Any classical shelves of a book shop or Amazon.

His writing depicts [among other things] all his conquests and is truly a must in all organised behaviour, management, logical thinking and communication. I've read most of his writing 5 times and I can't recommend it enough. Not a wrinkle of age transpires through the clear, concise, eloquent and logical logic of Julius's prose. A good idea for a Xmas present!

entry date: 10.12.00

345. "Lust For Life"

Dear Diary,

Lust doesn't come that easily; especially when you're living in a big city. Not lust as in sexual drive, lust as in love for life. If misery is a part of me, then I'll be a milestone deep down, down in a fountain of tears, crying out all my desperation. Thanks Heavens my immune system automatically releases some toxins to my brain cells, which in turn coerce a reaction from an equal and opposite force: anger. [From anger to love]

I always react with anger and this is an automatic self-defence. This protects me and enhances my lust for life. I don't care much for all this stuff about destroying one's karma. In my case it invigorates my inner and outer self, soothes me and delivers a new energy. A constant re-birthing. I always feel like I was doing the twelve tasks of Hercules. [The Greek guy] or Asterix for that matter. [The twelve tasks of Asterix.] An account of 12 challenges makes a fascinating read.

[For both adults and children.] Another Great Xmas gift.

 [Not to mention the comics and the staggering games.]

entry date: 11.12.00

346. "EuroCrap"

Dear Diary,

"The largest summit in EU history was held in Nice, France (and still running) and is another waste of time." A bunch of elected pompous wankers reunited all on one roof to play the fart to get. Squandering what one million, two of taxpayer's money in the process? This certifies the fact that we are paying too many taxes; much too much judging by this sheer scale of debility.

Haggling and harsh negotiations don't get anyone anywhere. Go back home, relax and rethink. There could be only one winner. Europe.

The worst news ever is that the former Eastern countries won't be able to join or "free trade" for another 10 years. Clumsy Oafs! Don't they know that by lack of trade and exchanges, instead of getting richer, they will barge their way through by any means necessary whilst their economy will sink and sink further?

This new nation of refugees has been created by Europe and will cost billions of monies in instability. One must ask oneself why and how the Roman Empire collapsed!

This has not been a Xmas present.

entry date: 12.12.00

347. "Sue you, Sir!"

Dear Diary,

London in England is a great place to be for anachronisms, folklore and broken communication. This is the chaos that attracted me to this pretentious hole in the first place. So, who am I to disagree?

Communication and chaos come to a price!

This has been a Xmas present.

entry date: 13.12.00

348. "Mea Culpa "

Dear Diary,

Well, I'm guilty. Guilty of misleading users or simply confusing them.

But it's true. It's all true!

If I have said in the past that I'm working with a gang of tosspots, I've never implied [in a million years] that the tosspots in question were either the people I work with, clients, my Dearest users or my record labels. Though my labels and the one in waiting are tosspots. A bunch of lousy accountants too scared of the next best thing to come.

I've been told off by the Labour Party for spreading too many rumours about them and by confusing issues. I may refrain from expressing my anger in the future, but I'm certainly not confusing ISSUES. As the real issues are never tackled and things rarely ever change. **Revolutions don't work.** Only EVOLUTION. But it's too slow. Far too slow. Too many people suffer in the process. We are making a difference by saying things that matter. We cover, we debate, we move on. They don't.

That reminds me: I went to the pictures [movie] last night. I saw Small Time Crooks by Woody Allen. Tracey Ullman is tremendous. Playing common trash [allegedly]. I laughed. I'm a big fan of Woody. Zelig is a true masterpiece. I just bought it on DVD.

entry date: 14.12.00

349. "Stranded, Empty Handed"

Sorry Folks,

But I still think that London is the best place in the world, media wise to be in, after New York naturally. After years of privatisation of the Rail network, the whole system collapsed. Trains started to derail and in the year Y2K alone nearly 100 people died or were badly injured. The tube [subway] is improving after years of misery, delays and catastrophes. After too many derailments, the government finally [under public pressure] stepped in and ordered massive speed restrictions enabling the network to rebuild its 100 year old tracks.

As a result of speed restrictions, everyone is using the car, it's much, much cheaper. This is causing havoc in the streets. The air pollution is 40% beyond the barely acceptable level.

Continues tomorrow.

Link to save your soul:

Alchemy resources here: The <u>Iconologia</u> of <u>Cesare Ripa</u> was conceived as a guide to the symbolism in emblem books. It was very influential in the 17th century and went through a number of editions.

entry date: 15.12.00

350. "Stranded, Empty Handed (part 2)"

Sorry Folks,

Buses are another story altogether. They stop half-way through their journey for XYZ reasons. [diesel, lunch break, breakdown.] Now, they stop in the middle of nowhere, in the evening, in a dark alley-way. **Last night, the bus was full.** The reason given for stopping: heavy traffic. The bus was full up and a riot was looming. At the bus stop, about 50 passengers were already waiting, dumped from a previous journey. I got out of the storm and walked, walked for 25 minutes. No traffic, no one but some of my fellow passengers. [No lights, total darkness.]

There were at least eighty angry passengers rioting. Most definitely in other parts of London as well, people have been caught in similar circumstances. Another chaos completely ignored by Stagecoach, the bus operator and traditional media. Though, reports need to be marketed and that's precisely what I'm doing now. There is a world within a world and within it, another world bursting to get out.

Link to save your soul:

The X-files: compendium of constructive criticism, organised by season and episode.

entry date: 16.12.00

351. "The Red Planet "

Dear Diary,

I went to the cinema [as I like to call it] last night.

I went to see the Red Planet.

Not bad. There was a safe beginning and a disappointing end. Too rushed. I may have been the last person to see the film, but not least. Very contemporary. The idea that we may be able to breeze on Mars is not too far-fetched. Life indeed started on Mars, before life started on Earth. Mars influenced our grand civilizations.

It's only a theory, but I firmly believe in it. Something has happened on <u>Mars</u> and will happen again. It's all part of its fascination and it's more alive than the <u>moon</u>, but there is water on both. That is another game that will keep our little mind busy for the next 50 years. At least. I often go to <u>Mars</u>. I'm a data and I can't beam up and away higher and higher than that. **Sweet dreams!**

entry date: 17.12.00

352. "Gold Rush Victory"

Dear Diary,

George Bush is finally president of the most powerful country in the world.

He will take office soon. Soon cannot be soon enough. The agony was beyond tolerance. He has already named a black person as the head of his admin.

<u>He is not so bad after all</u>.

Everyone can move on now. Was it 40 or 50 the amount of Hollywood stars who moved to London to avoid a <u>Republican</u> term?

<u>Madonna</u> won't be back for a while because she's getting married in my native <u>Scotland</u> and a few more won't be back

either, judging by the amount of rubbish they brought along with them. [A lot became my new neighbour in London's Canary Wharf. They don't wish to be named right now, although rumours about their whereabouts are floating high.]

By not allowing a recount of the votes, the American Supreme Court may have ended this agony and the sinking of the last echelon of seriousness the U.S. once had but it has also tarnished its reputation.

One hates to imagine how much!

I would nonetheless agree that it had to end at some point.

entry date: 18.12.00

353. "Big Brother XMAS"

Dear Diary,

Yes, I didn't like Mr. Blair this year and I certainly won't like him now.

His new (beyond evil) plan is to record all phone calls, emails and website hits swarming in the UK.

We will all be under 24-hour surveillance.

Well, he'll have a field day with my emails.

And I think a lot more people will oppose him.

Freedom of speech doesn't come easily, but when it is taken

away from you, one would expect the violation to bounce back.

This has not been a XMAS present.

Link to save your soul:

Freedom of Being

For clear and concise literature

entry date: 19.12.00

354. "What Is This? (part 1)"

This is the story so far as described in the **Y2K book**. Available: 31/02/01.

This is a work of fiction. All of the characters, incidents, and dialogue, except for incidental references to public figures, products, or services are imaginary and we are not intended to refer to any living persons or to disparage any company's products or services.

This is the story of one virus, the **Y2K**.

The evil root of communication portrayed in the **Y2KDiary.com**.

On the first of January 2000 a new portal went on air and from then on every day at midnight throughout the first **Y2K** year a new diary entry was displayed. From the usual rant on the

Bitterness of Being, the rear side of the news, the latest on what media agencies had in store for us, words only meaning something on the web, the latest advertising slogan crucified and all the broken links.

Ends tomorrow.

This has been a XMAS present.

entry date: 20.12.00

355. "What is This? (part 2)"

Thousands of websites have been reviewed, some vanished and some lives on but either way a skeleton remains on the **Y2KDiary.com**, this is the story of Jane, Janet, Tom, and Nick (V.A. Virtual Alien) and their adventures in a different dimension.

This is a work of fiction and is intended for a mature audience.

The world beyond is in good hands.

[Don't miss the 31st of December 2000 Live Showcase!]

Yours truly,

Merry XMAS and Happy New Year (though it doesn't matter to us at all).

Tom Norwood, Nick Peterson (from London) and guest star writers from New York, ED, Jane D'Arbanville and Janet

Priest. Supervised by Alex Altman.

This has been an XMAS present.

entry date: 21.12.00

356. "Countdown to XMAS..."

0. Roaming over the XMAS non-sense. Switching off the traumas and pain over a year's worth of cracks in communication; cracks in the Y2K virus.

1. LUST. (An INVITATION).

It is all one needs during this festive season. After all, it's when Baby Jesus was born and there can't be any smoke without fire!

Continued tomorrow...

entry date: 22.12.00

357. "Countdown to XMAS... (part 2)"

2. There are two sides to each story.

3. GREED. OPENING.

Please, check behind the flower by clicking on it.

Continued tomorrow...

entry date: 23.12.00

358. "Countdown to XMAS... (part 3)"

4. Oral Sex.

Please, check behind the <u>flower</u> by clicking on it.

Continued tomorrow...

entry date: 24.12.00

359. "Countdown to XMAS..."

4b. I was living rough in the streets of London, once, for over 5 months when I was 13. **On the 24th**. From then on, this time of the year remained irrelevant for me. I know how it feels. I will never forget.

4c. <u>Full frontal erection</u>.

Continued tomorrow...

entry date: 25.12.00

360. "Countdown to XMAS..."

5. What people do is <u>up to them</u>.

Continued tomorrow...

entry date: 26.12.00

361. "Countdown to XMAS..."

6. Pause for <u>thoughts</u>.

Continued tomorrow...

entry date: 27.12.00

362. "Countdown to XMAS..."

7. Boost for <u>another go</u>.

Continued tomorrow...

entry date: 28.12.00

363. "7 DaysNonTheRicher"

<u>Here we go</u>.

7 days or seven sins later, leaving us seven days <u>NonTheRicher</u>. Whatever that means. We came [thus] far, so I might as well go on. We are slowly nearing the end of the <u>Y2KDiary</u>. But we did it. **Read on**. 31st, here I come! <u>The virus will finally strike</u>.

In the meantime, we might as well puke and repent the last seven days of one's life for we are doomed. **Repent sinner!**

On a final note of [de] preciation (the opposite of [a] preciation. Don't worry; we never pretended to make any sense at all whatsoever in here.) The amount of fur coats I bought on this XMAS didn't impress me.

Some were born equal, some were born more equal than others and some were born with mushy peas instead of a brain. Will anyone finally understand the meaning of life?

entry date: 29.12.00

364. "Not A Diary"

Dear Diary,

I had a strong disagreement with a friend of mine yesterday about the content of the diary, not being a diary and being one-sided.

Firstly, it is a diary because it reflects the year in chronological order and then, it cannot be one-sided merely because the user writes the diary. This represents some fresh thoughts of the day digested from the world's agonising whispers and my [and my fellow workers] daily trips to a different dimension.

This whole compound gathers together 200 000 users, although it has been rather quiet over XMAS despite an extensive campaign. Not growing but steady during the week and unevenly spread, usually around midnight. It's dead on Monday with the busiest time on Sunday evening. Unlike so many famous <u>dot.coms</u> well profiled in the media, gone today, we're still here.

So there!

entry date: 30.12.00

365. "Overwhelming Hypocrisy"

Dear Diary,

I've received an email about a new <u>queer company</u>.

I'm confused about their actual product content but full marks for the choice in slogan: "I'm queer. And by the way, this is not an apology." "No, white wedding, sorry mum."

Same sex kissing on billboards. This won't last. If a straight woman widely spread and openly available for Christian Dior (By the way, my body lotion is <u>Eau Sauvage</u>, from <u>Dior</u>) on billboard is forced out, queer propaganda can only be far too overwhelming for a nation still at loggerheads with their own hypocrisy. Anyway, gay weddings are about to become a fact of life in the "00" years.

entry date: 31.12.00

366. "The Last Diary Of The Year."

Dear Diary,

[I'm trembling] The last Diary of the year.

Something illusory, almost elliptical. <u>Only in the mind</u>. A scripture barely removable. A derogatory statement crammed from within.

<u>Julius Caesar</u> invented that damn calendar. Fuck Julius. Who the hell is he? Why does it have to end this way? <u>366</u> days later. It was a very long time that drifted almost invisibly. Cruel mantra. Where are you?

If the days lost can gain as much enthusiasm as the entire New Year's Eve put together then the story so described was perhaps worth living after all. <u>Minus the blunders</u>.

Happy New Year! (Even if you're not using this calendar)

Thank you for being there.

[But it doesn't have to end this way...]

<u>Go BACK IN TIME!</u>

Epilogue

After launching a search engine and a diary for the year 2000, we kept going with a new entry at midnight every day. Some entries were raw and unedited. We ended on the 31st of December 2009. We had enough. Some were good entries, many needed to be edited and I embarked on a painful path to edit all the entries from the first of January 2001 until the first of December 2009. We released 3 enormous books containing all the entries titled: Beyond the Sphere of Reasonable Doubt The very first edition (we had 6 in all) had to cover the cover of a tax filing account in the UK but we smudged blood all over it -I could have added sweat but it didn't look too good-. It wasn't real blood but it was to show that it has not been easy, sometimes bloody even -figuratively speaking-. The cover of the third book had to embrace a film of the same name but with no relation, except that one diary entry was called this way and precluded the TV show.

If I was arrogant and pretentious I would say that The Y2K File: The Y2K Diary was a publishing phenomenon in the 21st century and in web terms, one can easily remain anonymous. I suppose a "phenomenon" is when the money follows and we didn't even know the website was a "phenomenon" until later. During its peak from January until early April, we discovered about 5 years later from the stats that it started gradually from 0 to thousands, hundreds of thousands, 100 million, 700 million, 8.... During that time our server provider automatically increased the access to our server, we didn't know that we signed up for this, if on the unlikely event that we had an "increased access' '. £200, £500, £1200, £5000 pounds for "shared servers' access" £10 000 and the invoices kept piling up, so did the direct debits in our bank account until the end of April then the bills started to slow down again. We were too busy running the diary entries of everything that was happening at the time, fed by a myriad of agencies and music labels who saw or "Submit an entry" form on the website. The diary entries were not that popular, only a few hundred thousand and it peaked at 2M, what attracted visitors was the Forum. This no doubt increased the costs. I only became aware back in 2005, from the CGI bin (the folder from the website) containing hundreds of thousands of emails. I assumed that it was the server provider who mixed up their database with our server. People dumped everything there: from a huge amount of items that I'm sure came from the then USENET site as they had similar stuff, all the ill deeds from the Church of Scientology with entire database of names, government departments memorandums, the Official Cornish language dictionary -we did a special entry on this- and the author wanted me to make it available for ever so we did, many entries are still available and web had a link to it from the Defra website and other places. Many small tech groups requested a feature and we were glad to oblige and many became very big like Slashdot. Yahoo was the dominant search engine but we advertised AltaVista and Amazon with a link. The only time Amazon paid something to anyone more than the minimum wage. Google was defined as small then, hard to believe.

Anyway, we operated a strict "**no-censorship**" policy so we became the trash of the internet. I never got any time to browse through the forum. The files were just too weird and dangerous to peruse through: it was the Dark Web. **We created freedom of expression** and at a price. It was like Napster 2000 sharing files. We did an entry with them but refused to enable a system that they offered to have Napster on The Y2K File with direct music exchange.